Like P

Ross thought. It felt so right, so good, holding her like this. His restless spirit seemed to find peace in Gloria's presence. And yet the sensations she stirred in him could not be termed as peaceful. Far from it. It was puzzling, these conflicting emotions. His feelings would have to be analyzed later—when he could think straight again. Right now all he wanted to do was be with her, hold her, kiss her....

He remembered she did not want to be kissed. Not by him, at least. She'd made that perfectly clear. Gazing down into her flushed face, he again felt that irresistible pull.

He lowered his head to bring his face closer to hers.

Dear Reader,

Welcome to Silhouette. Experience the magic of the wonderful world where two people fall in love. Meet heroines who will make you cheer for their happiness, and heroes (be they the boy next door or a handsome, mysterious stranger) who will win your heart. Silhouette Romances reflect the magic of love—sweeping you away with books that will make you laugh and cry, heartwarming, poignant stories that will move you time and time again.

In the next few months, we're publishing romances by many of your all-time favorites, such as Diana Palmer, Brittany Young, Emilie Richards and Arlene James. Your response to these authors and other authors of Silhouette Romances has served as a touchstone for us, and we're pleased to bring you more books with Silhouette's distinctive medley of charm, wit and—above all—*romance*.

I hope you enjoy this book and the many stories to come. Experience the magic!

Sincerely,

Tara Hughes
Senior Editor
Silhouette Books

MIA MAXAM

On Restless Wings

Published by Silhouette Books New York

America's Publisher of Contemporary Romance

The airforce wife is a special breed of woman—
proud, independent and dedicated—
and none of them are more special than
my mother, Gertrud Maxam.
Mama, thank you for always being there for me.

SILHOUETTE BOOKS
300 E. 42nd St., New York, N.Y. 10017

ISBN: 0-373-08513-3

First Silhouette Books printing June 1987

America's Publisher of Contemporary Romance

Printed in the U.S.A.

Books by Mia Maxam

Silhouette Romance

Race the Tide #205
Lost in Love #236
Loyal Opposition #324
Something Sentimental #450
On Restless Wings #513

MIA MAXAM

has been happily married for eighteen years to her husband Phil, an Air Force officer. With their two young daughters, they have just completed a tour of duty in Alaska, one of their favorite states. Although they move every three years, Mia says home is Malabar, Florida. A graduate of Florida Institute of Technology, Mia has a degree in Mathematics and continues to maintain an interest in the sciences.

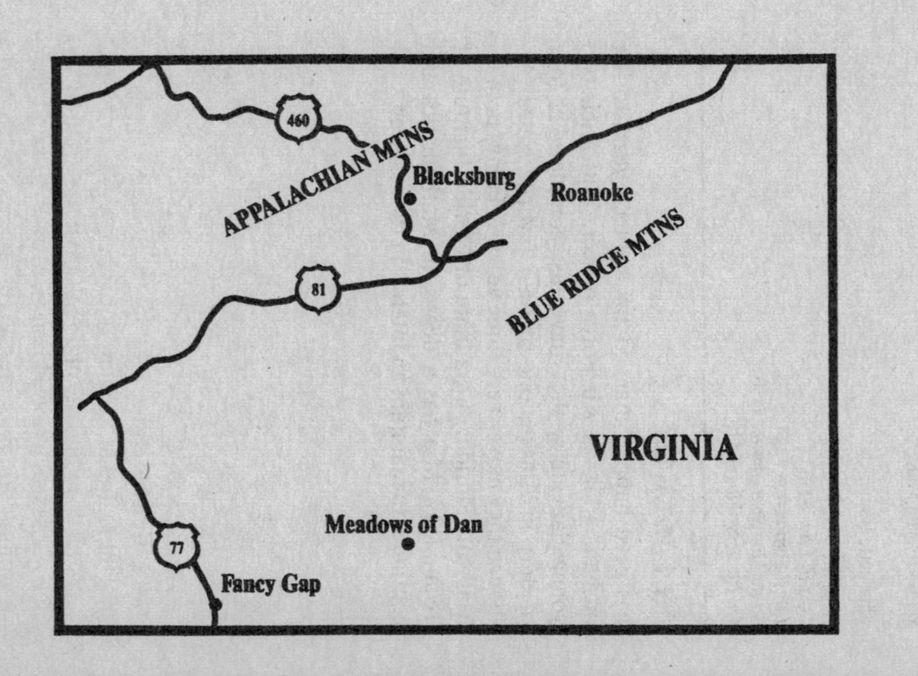
460
APPALACHIAN MTNS
Blacksburg
Roanoke
81
BLUE RIDGE MTNS
VIRGINIA
Meadows of Dan
77
Fancy Gap

Chapter One

The 220-horsepower Whirlwind engine had never run more smoothly, Ross Adams thought with satisfaction. The drone of the seven-cylinder, air-cooled engine was music to his ears. With the practiced eye of a veteran pilot, he scanned the blue-and-yellow wings of the 1935 Stearman biplane. He had been cruising at an altitude of five thousand feet for a little better than three hours. The pale winter sun was at its zenith. Below, like a silver river parting the rolling hills of southwestern Virginia, was Interstate 81. Due south were the Blue Ridge Mountains, home to towns with quaint names like Fancy Gap and Meadows of Dan.

After spending the night in Columbia, South Carolina, Ross had followed Interstate 77 up through North Carolina. With one eye on the altimeter, he banked to his left, then dropped to thirty-five hundred feet to follow Highway 460 on its northern route. On the horizon he could just make out the rounded tips of the Appalachian Mountains. The smoky gray landscape undulating beneath him brought to mind tales of Iroquois Indians and settlers wearing coonskin caps and leather moccasins. Daniel Boone. Davy Crockett. A civil war had been fought over this land. His gaze darted to the northwest. A front was heading his way, but if instincts served him correctly, he'd be on the ground before the late winter storm hit.

Ross liked flying by the seat of his pants, using the ground roads for navigation. More than one of his compatriots and fellow F-16 pilots back at McDill Air Force Base in Florida envied him this opportunity away from the rigors of modern warfare. Three months away from pulling air defense alerts when he lived in an alert hangar for seven days at a time, waiting for a call to intercept the enemy. Three months away from attending 4:00 a.m. briefings before routine missions and monotonous debriefings afterward. It was a difficult way of life.

And dangerous. That part of his work had never bothered Ross, but lately he'd been experiencing spells of vague unrest. Not with the job. With himself.

When the chance to substitute teach at a university came along, he'd grabbed at it. The regular instructor, an air force officer teaching at Virginia Tech's Reserve Officer Training Corps, was on a three-month convalescent leave. That meant Ross was committed for one quarter. At the end of that time, he knew he'd be itching to be back in the cockpit of his interceptor aircraft. A temporary change of pace was all he wanted.

In the meantime, Major Ross Adams would not be giving up flying. Restoring and piloting his pre-World War II biplane was more than a hobby. There was something about flying with the wind in his face and the scent of fuel oil filling his nostrils. Even the vibration of the engine gave him a deep sense of satisfaction. Slicing through the clouds and spiraling into the sun was like making love to a sensuous woman. There was nothing else like it in the world.

Ross turned his attention back to the Virginia landscape, a grayish-brown beneath March skies. He caught sight of the Blacksburg municipal airport—his destination, if fortune hadn't been on his side. The commanding officer at the university's military science department—his base for the next three months—had put him in touch with a realtor who had just what he was looking for: a private runway and hangar to house his prized Stearman. That the property had living quarters was an added bonus.

From the pocket of his well-worn leather jacket, he produced the letter from Carter Realty. He shifted his goggles to his forehead. Unfolding the piece of paper, he quickly reviewed the navigational instructions. Then keen blue eyes swept across the horizon to double-check his position.

A muffled sound came from the forward passenger cockpit. "You okay up there, Jane?" he called out. Jane was a trooper, and Ross took the silence that followed as an affirmative answer. "Not too much longer now, honey."

The plane's wings dipped to the right and the craft swung down, slicing through a wispy cloud. Ross searched for the landmarks specified in the letter. A water tower and a radio transmitter. Now if the realtor was correct, the landing strip should be just ahead, beyond a wooden hangar, its roof painted with the words Drink Mountain Dew.

And there it was! Ross made one trial pass over the airfield. It was grassy and smooth, just as the owner had written. A faded wind sock hung limply in the still winter air. Overlooking the runway was a neat white farmhouse nestled in an ancient apple orchard. Committing all this to memory in the space of a few seconds, Ross pulled back on the controls. The Stearman responded promptly and gained altitude before circling once more.

"Well, ready or not, Jane, down we go!" Ignoring the sounds from the other cockpit, he prepared to land.

The still air, heavy with late winter chill, sent an involuntary shiver down Gloria Russell's spine. Adjusting the lightweight earphones over her wool cap, she took long, steady strides. She could walk this path with her eyes closed, she realized as she instinctively sidestepped a fallen log. A good thing, too. The masculine voice on the tape player held her full attention.

"Random number generation...three million bytes...mathematical progression..." Greek to the average person, but vital information to the small, energetic woman with the soft brown eyes. Her straight black hair was completely hidden beneath a green knit cap. Under a gray down parka, she was dressed in a baggy gray warm-up suit.

Frosty puffs of breath marked each exhalation of air. A long walk every day kept her physically fit and her mind sharp, and that was important to her work, sedentary as being in front of a computer terminal was. Gloria marched on steadfastly, part of her mind on the tape, the other placing one foot in front of the other. When the tape ran out, she stopped. Stripping off her gloves, she turned the cassette over, eager to get to the information on the other side.

"Simulation programs in the design of educational tools..." Fascinated, Gloria trudged onward, hardly noticing that she had left the woods behind and was walking along the crest of an ancient mountain. To one side she could see the town of Blacksburg, home of Virginia Tech, where she worked as an associate professor. A crow cawed and caught Gloria's attention. The motley black bird was sitting on the shoulders of a decrepit scarecrow. Beyond the fallow garden was a farmhouse, deserted now, its former occupants having left in search of more stable employment in the city.

The two-story house reminded Gloria of the farm where she'd grown up not too many miles outside Blacksburg. She snapped off the tape, sank down onto a large rock and thought back to her beginnings. Gloria Russell's early years had undoubtedly been happy and full of laughter. But overriding all other memories were those of her mother going without a great many things just to make ends meet. In fact, it had not been easy for any of the six Russells. It was Gloria's opinion that her father should have sold the farm much sooner than he had. But he was a proud, hardworking man who did not readily admit defeat. And her mother—sweet, uncomplaining—was always eager to please her husband.

Gloria could not remember exactly when she decided she wanted things to be different when she grew up. She only knew that she would never let her life be controlled by the whims of man or nature. Her destiny would rest in her own two capable hands.

A brilliant student, she'd graduated from high school at sixteen, won a full scholarship to Virginia Tech, and graduated at nineteen with a degree in computer science. Another four years of work and research brought a Ph.D. in education and a full-time faculty position at Tech. She taught computer programming, but her specialty was documenting the development of contemporary computer technology. It was exciting to think that her penchant for gathering historical data was going to get her what she wanted most in life—tenure at Virginia Tech.

Only after that would she allow herself time to fill in the empty spaces in her life, perhaps find a suitable mate. A man with whom she could share her triumphs. A dependable man who possessed the same interests as she.

Erik Windom came to mind. Older than Gloria, he had achieved tenure some years back and was a full professor in the math department. With her teaching in the computer science department, there was no competition between them, yet their fields were similar enough to ensure common interests. Among the faculty, they were viewed as the perfect couple. Attractive, intelligent and sensible. Perhaps Erik was lacking in passion, but that trait was not high on Gloria's list of attributes in a partner. For now it was enough to enjoy Erik's company on their regular Saturday night dates or at the odd faculty get-together.

Anything more than that would have to wait. At this point in time she would allow nothing to come between her and her work.

With renewed determination she jumped to her feet and snapped on the tape. Revolutionary changes were occurring in the computer industry. Changes that were important to record. On sure footing, she made her way down the mountain. Many computer companies chronicled their own developments, but a comprehensive work on an international scale did not exist. For several years, Gloria had accumulated such data and had faithfully cataloged it in her computer. When she'd conveyed to her department head her intention of compiling it into a college text, he had enthusiastically urged her on. In fact, Dr. Mellon immediately put her in touch with Lafferty at MIT. And here she was, on a leave of absence to finish up her project.

She concentrated as Dr. Lafferty launched into a new topic. "One of the latest computer languages is called Ada. Named after the first woman programmer. Not in common use as of this date, it has been predicted Ada will be the most widely used computer language in this country by the year 2000. The defense department has already adopted it due to its..."

The path in the woods branched, and Gloria automatically took the fork that led to the remodeled farmhouse she rented from Carter Realty. Intent on the tape, she strode across the property's unused airfield, a leftover from the days when there were enough working farms in the area to support a local crop duster.

A rackety noise intruded on her thoughts. Gloria glanced up. She couldn't believe her eyes! A biplane was bearing down on her, its loud engine roaring like an angry swarm of bees. The machine was scarcely twenty feet away and closing in fast. To avoid being clipped in the head by the edge of a bright yellow wing, Gloria's instinct prompted her into a running dive. At that instant, the plane swerved, missing her by a good three yards.

Too late, though, to stop her plunge into a pile of melted snow. The tape player flew out of her pocket, became disconnected from the headphones and skittered across a frozen patch of brown grass. A few feet away, Gloria found herself facedown in mud. Behind her, the aircraft rolled to an ungainly halt.

She heard a shout and the pounding of footsteps. "Are you okay?" a man's voice called down to her anxiously.

Gloria raised her head. The first thing she noticed about the man bending over her was that he had the most incredible blue eyes she had ever seen. The second thing she noticed was his antiquated leather flying cap with the goggles pushed up over his forehead. The tip of his nose was red from the cold, and his mouth was tight-lipped with concern.

"Let me help you up." A gloved hand reached out and assisted Gloria to her feet.

The sky-blue eyes swept over her muddy figure. Still winded from her fall, Gloria could only stare back at him. His brown leather bomber jacket, zipped to his chin, matched the leather cap. An edging of red material peeked out around his neck. Further inspection showed long, lean legs encased in tan wool slacks.

"That was a stupid thing to do, running out in front of my plane like that!"

Gloria's eyes widened. She jerked her arm out of the stranger's grasp.

"Stupid!" she exclaimed hotly. "What do you think you were doing, landing that machine out there! You could have killed someone!"

A light flared in his eyes, and he stepped away from her. "No kidding!" He pointed to the worn canvas cone. "You see that, kid? That's a wind sock." He shifted his arm. "Over there is a hangar. And that is called an airplane." He spoke as if she were dim-witted. "If you'd been paying attention instead of listening to rock music on that headset, you'd have heard the sound of my engine. It's kind of hard to miss."

Gloria became painfully aware of how she looked, standing in the middle of the field with mud splattered all over her bulky jacket. The knees of her sweatpants were wet and dirty. Her knit cap was askew. The headphones were still in place, but the connector end was dangling uselessly beneath her chin.

"I know what an airplane is, mister, and I was not listening to... oh, never mind!" Why should she explain what was on the tape to this... this reject from a World War I movie! "I'm still among the living, no thanks to you, so why don't you get back in the cockpit and wing it out of here? You're trespassing on private property." To her horror, her voice came out thin and squeaky and her nose started to itch.

"No thanks to me!" he huffed. "If I weren't such a good pilot, you'd be dead meat, kid!"

At the look in his eyes, Gloria took a step away from the man. A shaft of pain shot up her leg. It would serve him right, she thought, if he'd caused her to break an ankle. He caught the wince of pain in her eyes—the only part of her face that was actually visible besides her mouth and nose.

"Hey, kid, you *are* hurt!" The anger changed swiftly to concern, and he made a move toward her.

She put up a hand. "No, no. I'm okay," she insisted and stood her ground.

"Where do you live? I'll help get you home."

She straightened to her full five-foot-one-inch height. "I am perfectly capable of getting home on my own. I just want to make sure you get out of here first."

He frowned. "I'm only going as far as the hangar over there, but your concern for my plane is touching."

She ignored his sarcasm. "What do you mean, you're going to the hangar?"

Once again he treated her as if she had taken leave of her senses—or never had any to start. "I mean that I'm going to taxi the Stearman over to that building and get inside before the snowstorm hits." He spoke very slowly.

Gloria looked over her shoulder at the darkening sky. She had been so preoccupied that she had not noticed the change of weather. A cold wind gusted across the field. It penetrated her wet clothing. She suppressed the urge to scratch her nose and sniffed instead.

"You can't park that monstrosity in there. It's private property." A loud sneeze punctuated her words.

"It's okay, kid," the man told her. "I have permission from the owner."

"You what?" It was hard to sound indignant with a drippy nose. Reaching into her coat pocket, she sneezed again. Where was her handkerchief?

"Gesundheit." With an impatient movement, the man produced a clean square of cloth from his back pocket. "Here, use this." About to decline, she was interrupted by a second sneeze. The handkerchief was unceremoniously thrust into her hands. Throwing away her pride, she opened it and smothered another ignominious sound.

"You'd better get home and have your mother fix you a hot toddy before you catch pneumonia."

Gloria's eyes widened. "Listen here, mister. I'm not a baby who has to run home to Mommy!" Her words were muffled by the handkerchief.

"Whatever you say..." He made as if to turn away.

"I say you've landed in the wrong field!" She waved the wadded-up hanky skyward. "I'm sure they all look alike from up there."

The man turned back to her slowly. Blue eyes narrowed menacingly. "I've been flying planes for a good fifteen years, and I assure you that I don't make mistakes like that." When he spoke again, his voice came out more gently. "Listen, kid, I admire your concern for a neighbor. If it makes you feel any better, you can call Carter Realty. I'm renting this hangar and the upstairs apartment of that farmhouse over there from Mrs. Carter. Now, I have things to do before that storm hits."

He turned away and missed Gloria's gasp of surprise. "Mrs. Carter!"

"That's the lady." He spoke over his shoulder without altering his stride toward the idling biplane. "She'll vouch for me." And he jumped agilely into the open air cockpit. With a jaunty wave, he revved the engine and taxied the craft toward the hangar.

The man acted as if he owned the very earth beneath his aircraft! It rankled Gloria.

Ignoring the fact that her ankle felt distinctly sore, she shot across the field as if the devil were after her. That man—under the same roof!

Inside the house, she stomped through the mudroom and into the kitchen, tossing the headphones and her hat onto the table. Jerking the telephone receiver off the wall, she dialed Margie Carter's office. The line was busy.

She slammed the receiver down and stomped back to the mudroom and stripped off her gloves, parka and boots. Her ankle throbbed, but she ignored it. In her bedroom she fairly flew out of her clothes. A pair of jeans and a clean, dry sweater replaced the wet articles. These she gathered up and, back in the mudroom, stuffed them into the washer. Through the window over the washer, Gloria could see the man moving about in the hangar. The bomber jacket was unzipped. Gloria caught the distinct flash of a scarlet muffler around his neck.

"The Red Baron," she hissed. "The man thinks he's the Red Baron!" Turning away indignantly, she looked down and caught sight of his snowy white handkerchief crumpled on the floor. She stooped to pick it up. Another sneeze caught her and she was forced to stifle it into the cloth.

It was back to the kitchen. She made a beeline for the wall phone. With angry fingers, she dialed the number for Carter Realty. As she waited for the circuits to connect, she leaned her head back against the wall. The movement jostled a large decorative piece of wood carved in the shape of a key and mounted next to the phone. The jangling noise struck a chord in Gloria's memory.

"Oh, no!" She moaned out loud and slammed the receiver back in place. Her eyes fixed on a hook where a lone key was suspended. If memory finally served her correctly, Margie had put that key there just last week. Gloria had been so involved with her work that she had paid scant attention to her sister as she had breezed into Gloria's apartment with the key and—

And a note! Margie had handed her a note so that Gloria wouldn't forget—forget what? She charged into the large spare bedroom, which had been converted into an office and computer room. Gloria prided herself on being a disciplined, organized person. And that characteristic was apparent everywhere except her desk. Frantic hands searched the jumble of papers, books and diskettes scattered across the oak surface.

A scrap of crumpled paper caught her eye, and she fished it out of the chaos. There it was, in plain black and white, on Carter Realty stationery.

"Gloria," she read out loud, "show upstairs apartment to R. Adams. Arrives March 13."

Well, that settles it, she thought smugly, flinging the note down. Today was only the... Her eyes flew to the calendar on the wall. The thirteenth! Her groan was drowned out by a loud knock on the back door.

Chapter Two

With her luck, it was probably Friday the thirteenth! But no. Another glance at the calendar verified that it was only Thursday. Gloria's attention shifted back to the note in her hand. Margie wanted her to show the upstairs apartment to a prospective tenant. It sounded simple enough, she told herself as she hurried back to the kitchen. An ordinary task. But that man out there was no ordinary man. And it had sounded as if he had already decided to take the apartment, sight unseen.

More knocking interrupted her thoughts. "The door is open," she called out as she dialed Margie's number again.

Waiting for the circuits to connect, she tried to remember everything she could about the vacant living quarters above her. Margie had bought the farm more than a year ago. Impressed with the remodeling results, Gloria had become her sister's first tenant, moving in as soon as the work on the downstairs apartment had been completed. But due to a chronic lack of funds on Margie's part, the work on the upstairs had come to a temporary halt. During the past six months, workmen had appeared at the house only sporadically, their arrivals coinciding with the times Margie received a commission from a sale. Divorced with two children to care for, Margie needed the income another tenant would bring in, and her goal was to get the second apartment in tip-top condition.

Just how tip-top, Gloria had no idea. She'd been far too involved with her own work to pay attention. And look where that had gotten her. A near miss and a sore ankle, not to mention the mortification of being plucked from a mud puddle by a man who was too attractive for his own good.

She heard footsteps in the mudroom. "I'm on the phone!" she called out.

Ross followed the lilting voice to the kitchen doorway. Halting, he stared at the girl with her back to him. Dark-haired and petite, she was dressed in an oversize sweater the color of ripe lemons. His eyes drifted downward in appreciation of striped blue jeans molding a pair of very shapely legs. Her feet were encased in thick woolen socks, but she wore no shoes. One small foot impatiently tapped the floor.

"Still busy!" she huffed and quickly returned the receiver to its cradle before whirling around to face the newcomer.

Ross's gaze swung upward. Halfway back to her exquisite face, he realized that she was not a girl. With curves and valleys in intriguing places, she was a woman who could take a man's breath away.

Including his. Clearing his throat, Ross noted the pink in her cheeks and how the color contrasted sharply with her creamy ivory skin. And her eyes, he thought as he met her gaze, were the most unusual shade of brown. Brandy, he decided, flecked with an intoxicating shade of gold.

"Hello," he said. "I'm Ross Adams. I believe you were expecting me."

His bright blue eyes seemed iridescent in his tanned face. Chapped cheeks and nose would not ordinarily enhance a man's looks, but this fellow fairly glowed with health and vitality. Obviously he did not follow the rules. Standing tall and straight and seemingly unaffected by their close encounter, he irritated Gloria.

"No," she responded to his innocent remark, "but then you already discovered that."

"I beg your..." Blue eyes narrowed as he looked closer at the small defiant woman. High cheekbones accented her short straight nose. A nose that seemed familiar...

"My recorder!" The woman exclaimed suddenly. Ross glanced from her to the tape machine sticking out of his jacket pocket. At the same moment, she suppressed a sneeze into a large white handkerchief. His handkerchief.

"Why, you're the—"

She sneezed again. "Yes," Gloria admitted, dismayed at the thought of coming down with a late-winter cold. "The kid with the Walkman." Unwavering, her eyes held his.

Somewhere along the way, Ross Adams had discarded the flying cap. Windblown, his hair was light brown and streaked with errant veins of gold. It was cut shorter than the current fashion—a maverick all the way, was Gloria's observation.

"I can hardly believe that you're the same person," Ross Adams was saying in his smooth, deep voice. He did not bother to hide the fact that he liked what he saw.

Mr. Macho himself, Gloria thought to herself.

Out loud, she addressed his remark. "I'll probably never be the same again, either."

One gold-tipped brow quirked upward. He did not pretend to misunderstand her. "I guess I didn't make a good impression out there."

"No, you didn't," she agreed in a deceptively innocent tone. "But just think, I now know the difference between a hangar and a wind sock. And the next time I see a machine with wings, I'll know it's called an airplane."

Ross thought back to how he'd chewed her out. "I deserve that," he admitted slowly.

"That and more," she retorted, thinking of the way he'd looked at her when he thought she wasn't paying attention.

"I'm normally a little more subtle. But you did startle me out there."

"Somehow, I think *subtle* is one word that's not in your vocabulary."

Her comeback, said in that soft, sweet voice, delighted him. She was right. He had a tendency to come on strong. A slow smile spread across his face.

The smile, revealing his slightly crooked white teeth, was totally unexpected. And so was Gloria's reaction to it. As his eyes crinkled and turned warm, she felt her breath stop short.

"It's a good thing I'm coming back to school this quarter," he reflected. Head tilted boyishly to one side, he regarded Gloria with steady blue eyes.

Too calculating, she decided quickly. Yet the amazing thing was that his wiles seemed to be working. Since when was she susceptible to masculine sweet-talk? she wondered as she gazed back at him. Why, her pulse was pounding at her temples, and her hands were distinctly clammy. Worse yet, her cheeks felt as if they'd encountered a flash fire. Under the guise of pushing a lock of black hair from her forehead, she checked for fever. Of course—all that sneezing and sniffling. She was coming down with the flu. As if to confirm her diagnosis, she sneezed again.

With his handkerchief pressed to her nose, she turned to take the key from its hook. "You can leave the recorder over there. The apartment's this way." Ross followed her out the door and up the staircase at the other end of the mudroom.

She glanced back at the man sporting the red scarf. "You said you're going back to school. I take it you mean Tech?"

"Yes." He pulled off his gloves and stashed them in the pocket of his leather jacket.

"Graduate school?"

"Don't I wish those days were back!" The blue eyes twinkled. "No, I'll be teaching military science at the air force detachment."

Gloria was not surprised to learn he was a military man. Virginia Tech had a long proud history as a military school, and despite the fact that it had been coed for years, the Corps of Cadets was still popular with the students, men and women alike. "Isn't that unusual, coming in during the last quarter of the year?"

"Yes," Adams agreed with Gloria. "One of the officers was put on convalescent leave until June. I'll be taking his place in the classroom until then."

Reaching the top landing, Gloria turned toward him. "So you'll only need the apartment for a short time."

"Yes. I explained all that to Mrs. Carter."

"Did she explain to you that the upstairs apartment isn't completely ready for a tenant?"

"Yes." He shrugged. "Between my work and my flying, I don't spend much time at home. I'm more concerned with having a clean, dry place to keep the Stearman."

"I see." Gloria inserted the key. The door, old and warped, did not budge.

"Here, let me," Ross offered. He stepped up beside her. Immediately she was enveloped in his scent, a mixture of fresh air and spicy cologne. The faintest hint of aviation fuel merely added to his appeal. He was not a tall man, but with strong broad shoulders that made short work of the sticky door, and a lean physique, he gave the illusion of height.

Pushing the door wide open, Ross stepped aside and motioned Gloria in ahead of him. He followed close behind, then walked purposefully to the center of the unheated room. With hands on slim hips, he turned a full circle, his keen eyes missing nothing.

Gloria had never known a person to dominate a room as this man did. The essence of him seemed to fill the empty spaces of the apartment that was cluttered with buckets, brushes, paint cans, sawhorses and assorted building supplies. With long strides, Ross Adams crossed to the kitchen area, his booted feet making a drumming noise across the scuffed, paint-splattered oak flooring. The sound echoed in the room.

Gloria imagined how it would sound one floor below. Distracting, to say the least. A nuisance was more likely. Gloria watched as he walked around the living area. He wore authority as easily as he sported the red scarf dangling about his neck. A complex man. Intelligent, a smooth talker, certainly a ladies' man and probably a heartbreaker. In the short time since he'd appeared on the scene, Gloria had learned that he was quick-tempered, with a tendency to jump to conclusions. Add to that a supreme confidence in himself as a man, a man who knew exactly what he wanted. He was arrogant and no doubt a daredevil, considering the type of transportation he favored. A military officer, he was used to giving orders. The very idea of sharing the farmhouse and its grounds with him—

"As you can see, the place is a mess," Gloria announced, abruptly cutting off her own thoughts. Why should she worry about Ross Adams, anyway? If her instincts served correctly, he was a man who sought the finer things in life—never mind what he said about his Stearman coming first. A man like him would never want to live in a place like this. In short order, he'd be back in that crate of his, flying out of her life as quickly as he had appeared.

Too bad, though, Gloria thought as she watched Ross Adams nod in agreement. Margie needed the money.

"It definitely needs some work," he remarked, checking a window frame. With the tips of his long fingers, he tapped at a gray-tinted wall.

"It wouldn't take much to make it livable." Loyalty to her sister made Gloria speak up. "A coat of primer, a bright color on the walls. A little paint remover and some varnish would do wonders for the floor." She looked around quickly. The place wasn't really that bad. "There's a new bathtub and sink."

Ross turned toward her and in the process bumped his head on the sloped ceiling. "Ouch!"

"The slant gives the place character," was Gloria's hasty remark.

Ross rubbed his head. "That's another way of putting it."

"The kitchen is really nice," she said brightly. "All new appliances." Ignoring the twinge in her ankle, she darted to open the oven door.

Ross followed more slowly. "Compact," he said, looking around.

He hates it, Gloria translated. "The washer and dryer down in the mudroom is for both tenants." The cold from the floor was beginning to radiate up her legs. She suppressed a shiver and wished she'd taken the time to put on shoes.

"There's the question of furniture. . . ."

He wasn't going to get the best of her at this point in the game, Gloria decided as her mind scrambled for an answer. "In the hangar. There are all kinds of things stored up in the loft. Ms. Carter had the stuff moved out there before she started the remodeling."

Taking care not to bump his head again, Adams moved to look out of the dormer-style window.

"That's a great view of the hangar and airstrip," Gloria added.

He was silent, then turned to face her. "It will do."

"What will do?" She'd been trying to anticipate his next objection and his comment caught her by surprise.

"The apartment. It will do fine." Decisively, he strode to the kitchen counter, pulling a slim leather book from his jacket pocket. In moments, he was handing her a signed check. "That should cover the first and last month's rent plus a deposit for damage."

If her math was up to par, he was paying almost double the amount she paid for her unfurnished two-bedroom unit.

"What's the matter?" he asked. "Isn't it enough?"

"Oh! No! I mean, I don't know." The man must think she was an absolute idiot, Gloria thought dismally, then plunged headlong into an explanation. "You see, I don't normally do this. I mean, rent out apartments. I'm just another tenant. Well, not just another tenant." By now the man was surely convinced she was not all right in the head! Closing her eyes for a quick moment, she gathered her thoughts. "I'm Margie Carter's sister, and she asked me to show you the place. And I'm not doing too good a job." Her final words were punctuated with a heavy sigh of frustration.

"You're doing just fine, Miss, uh, Carter, is it?"

"No. It's Russell. Gloria Russell. I'm not married." She wished the words back as soon as they were uttered. Now he'd think she was making it known that she was interested in him as a man. Interested and available.

Ross Adams was smiling at her. "Well, it's nice to meet you, Miss Gloria Russell." He extended his hand in a friendly gesture, and Gloria found she could not help but return his smile. Slowly, she put her hand in his. "Being neighbors," he went on, "we'll be seeing a lot of each other, I'm sure." Pleasure lit his eyes.

His firm touch set off a chain reaction that started in Gloria's fingertips, spread through her palm and glazed at the speed of light along her arm.

An alarm went off in her head, and her smile faded. The shortness of breath she was experiencing was not the flu! It was Ross Adams. The man was an undeniable danger to her peace of mind. Attractive, with a winning way about him, he had the potential to become a distraction in her life. And a distraction was something she most certainly did not need, not at this critical point in time. Her work was the only thing she should be thinking of.

"No!" Gloria pulled her hand away from his. For the first time in her life, she wished she had more experience in dealing with the opposite sex. Never one to mince words, she decided to be direct and go with the truth.

"Mr. Adams—"

"Ross."

"Mr. Adams." Glaring at him, she realized he wasn't going to make this easy. "Please don't get the wrong idea. I mean, I'm very glad to have rented out

Margie's apartment, but... Well, Margie is the one who needs a tenant, not me." Her eyes widened with horror at her own choice of words. She hurried on to explain. "What I mean is, I'm not in realty. I'm a professor at Tech, but I'm on leave of absence to work on a very important project. A text on the history of... But that's not important. The point is, having a close neighbor is not part of the plan and—"

She was relieved when he broke in. "And you don't want me to get the wrong idea." His look was thoughtful. "I presume the material on that tape wasn't rock music."

"Right."

"Well, Professor? Doctor?" She nodded at the latter. He looked her straight in the eye. "The bad news is that I'll be moving in tomorrow morning. The good news is that I will make a point to respect your privacy. I promise I won't disturb you. In fact, I'll be so quiet, you won't even know I'm up here."

"I'd appreciate that," Gloria replied slowly and took a step away from him. Was the man crazy? Had he never taken a good look at himself in the mirror? Had he ever listened to his own voice, so deep, with a caressing quality to its tone? With that short, gilded hair and those incredible sky-blue eyes, not to mention a very attractive dimple in his right cheek, a woman would have to be dead not to be disturbed when Ross Adams was around.

And you, dear girl, Gloria informed herself as she folded the check he had written, are very much alive.

She sneezed. Ross was immediately at her side, taking her by the elbow.

"Now that that's settled, Dr. Russell, I'm going to get you back into that warm kitchen of yours. I'll personally make you a cup of something hot to drink."

She darted him a quick look.

"No ulterior motives," he assured her. "It's the least I can do after practically running you over." He closed the door to the apartment behind them and pocketed the key.

"But that was my fault!" Gloria protested. "I should have looked where I was—"

"No, no," he insisted as they descended the stairs. "I accept full responsibility. And if you get pneumonia as a result, I'll never forgive myself."

She entered the kitchen ahead of him, taking care with her ankle. He pulled out a chair.

"Sit right here. How does tea sound?" he asked as he took the whistler off the stove and filled it with water from the tap.

"Wonderful," she had to admit. "It's in the glass canister next to the stove." An assortment of mugs hung on a tree next to the tea. Ross dropped a tea bag into a mug.

"Aren't you going to have some?"

"No," he answered firmly. "I'm only going to stay long enough to see that you're okay."

"But—"

"No buts. Well—" he grinned "—only one. Would you mind if I used your phone for a minute?"

"Of course I don't mind."

"Thanks. I just need to check in with my unit."

"The phone's on the wall."

He quickly made his call. "Sergeant Murphy! Major Adams here." There was a pause. "Thanks, Sarge, good to be here." Ross leaned one shoulder against the wall and kept an eye on the simmering kettle. "Put me through to Captain Stanek, would you?...Stek! Good to hear your voice! Listen, did Cadet Sands get in with my truck?...Great, how soon can he pick me up?...Sure, an hour will be fine. Just a minute and I'll get you directions." He turned to Gloria. "Dr. Russell? Could you give my friend navigational instructions to the farm?"

"Be glad to." Coming to her feet, she crossed to the phone. As she gave the captain instructions on how to find the farm, she watched her new neighbor efficiently pour steaming water into the waiting mug. After making sure the man at the other end of the line understood her directions, she handed the receiver back to Ross Adams.

Trying hard not to limp, she returned to her seat and savored the scent of the tea steeping in her mug. Waiting for it to cool, she lifted her wool-garbed foot onto the bottom rung of the chair. Absently she rubbed the sore ankle.

"See you, Stek," Ross was saying. Hanging up, he turned to survey the warm country kitchen with its red brick walls and beamed ceiling where green plants and copper pots vied for attention.

"Nice place," he commented, then shot a look Gloria's way. "Why are you doing that?"

Gloria looked up to find his eyes focused on her ankle. "Doing what?"

"Rubbing your leg. Are you sure you didn't get hurt when you fell out on the airstrip?" He took a step toward her.

"No damage done, really—"

"I'll be the judge of that." His voice was authoritative. In the next moment, he was crouching in front of her, firmly brushing her hands away. Off came her sock. Gloria froze as he lifted her pant leg out of the way. His large warm hands touched her ankle very gently.

"There's a bruise here!" he exclaimed softly. "Did I do that?" Concerned eyes demanded an answer.

"I must have twisted it when I fell. But I'll be fine, really." And she meant it. The throbbing was beginning to subside now that they were in the warm room.

But Ross was not satisfied. "Does this hurt?" He moved his fingers to the ankle.

"Just a little," Gloria whispered and closed her eyes, but not against any pain. The feel of his hands on her foot was strangely personal and more than a little unsettling. But then he'd unsettled her from the first moment they'd crossed paths.

"My friends will be here shortly with my truck. I can take you to the hospital."

"No! It's not that bad, Major Adams!"

He looked her full in the eyes. "A leg injury is not something you want to neglect, Dr. Russell. A few years ago, I was in an accident, and I remember being very stubborn about being taken to the hospital."

"Stubborn? You?" The corners of her lips quirked upward.

"Guilty as charged," he admitted, and his eyes crinkled in response.

"What kind of accident was it?"

He looked down to massage her foot. "Plane crash." His lips tightened almost imperceptibly, but Gloria caught the movement.

"Oh, I'm sorry!" she exclaimed quickly. "I didn't mean to bring back bad memories."

"It's not such a bad memory." He sat back on his haunches, one hand moving to her heel, the other rubbing her toes. "It was touch and go at first. I was flying an F-16 fighter aircraft. I dead-sticked it and brought her down on a strip of highway." As he spoke, he kneaded the arch of her foot. "The only casualty was a half-mile length of wire fence."

"And your leg," Gloria reminded him. His fingers were working magic on her feet.

"Yes," he agreed. "But I walked away from the accident. Actually, hobbled is a more accurate description." His slow grin was contagious.

"What happened to the plane?" Gloria leaned forward slightly, totally caught up in his story.

"It was recovered and overhauled. I flew her on at least two dozen more successful missions." There was no mistaking the pride in his voice.

"Why didn't you eject instead of taking a chance with your life?"

"I'd been flying over a heavily populated area. The thought of ejecting never entered my mind." He shrugged. His hands moved upward to her ankle. "I'm an excellent pilot and I knew I could bring her in."

"Are all pilots so confident?"

Her wry question brought a laugh from Ross. "No doubt! As I recall, it's part of the curriculum in pilot training class. Ego 101."

The blue eyes twinkled, and Gloria found herself laughing with him. "But seriously," he added, "a pilot without an ego wouldn't last long. A healthy share of confidence is a necessary ingredient in an aviator's makeup. You have to believe in yourself, in the rigorous training we go through. A pilot puts his faith in the aircraft and the mechanics that work on her. I might be alone in the cockpit, but flying a high-powered jet takes teamwork. I make the time to know my team, and when I take that bird up, I know that everyone has done nothing less than their best." His eyes glowed with sincerity.

"It's a very dangerous way of making a living," Gloria noted quietly.

"Yes," Ross acknowledged. "Very. Confidence and a sense of reality go hand in hand." He was no longer laughing.

"Don't you ever think of quitting?" She felt a fierce desire to know more about this fascinating man. "After all, you've already had one close call. I don't know if I could get back in the cockpit after an experience like that."

"I'm a professional," he explained. "I'm deeply committed to my career as a military pilot. I'd be half a man if I ever had to give it up." The lines of his face were etched with pride and determination.

"Were you in Vietnam?"

"Yes. It was my very first assignment out of flight school. I went over there filled with the idealism of youth and the conviction that what I was doing was right for our country." He sighed. "Like that of every other Vietnam vet, the course of my life was changed by the war." He looked up at Gloria. "Not dramatically. Just quietly." A light flared in his eyes. "But listen to me! We've known each other for less than an hour, and here I am, boring you with war stories!"

"Just one more question," Gloria insisted. "What's a fighter pilot doing in Blacksburg? It's a far cry from the real air force."

"That's true." Something flickered across his face, alerting Gloria to the fact that there was more to his story than he was telling. "The job sounded interesting, so I volunteered."

"Maybe you'll find out at the end of the three months that you like teaching."

Ross nodded seriously. "I'm sure I'll like it. But nothing could ever replace flying. At the end of the spring quarter, I'll be back in the cockpit of my F-16." His voice was filled with conviction. A special kind of feeling radiated from him as he spoke. It was a vibrant energy that almost reached out and caught Gloria in its sparkle, quickening her blood where he still touched her skin.

"Flying." Ross spoke the word with reverence. "It's what I wanted to do as far back as I can remember. There's nothing to compare it to, you know." Their eyes met. "Streaking through a blue sky, traveling higher and higher toward a burning sun. Sometimes I feel like I could just reach out and touch the flames." His words made it easy for her to imagine, and Gloria's senses became heightened. A vibrant silence filled the room.

The ringing of the telephone broke the spell that gripped them both. He dropped his hands from her foot, and she rose slowly to go to the phone. "Yes," she said into the mouthpiece, "thank you, I'll ready the terminal." Hanging up, she turned to Ross. "Excuse me for just a moment; I've got a transmission coming in and I have to set up my computer." She disappeared down a hallway.

Ross rose and watched her go. There was something about the woman. He found himself wanting to open up to her, to make her understand what made him tick. That was not normal for him—the urge to get close to another person, especially a woman. Not that he didn't like intimacy with the right woman. But to confide in a person of the opposite sex? That was a no-no for him. Confidences led to deeper feelings. And deeper feelings led to commitments. Ross sighed and ran harried fingers through his hair.

He had a prior commitment to his career. Personal experience had shown him that there was no room for a woman in the scheme of his life. Long ago, after returning home from Vietnam, he'd decided that if he wanted to fly, he'd have to do it alone. No wife to complicate his life, no children to leave behind if he didn't come home from work one day. He'd seen what that had done to the families of some of his buddies. Buddies that had not come home from Vietnam.

"There," she said, announcing her return. "The phone will ring, then it'll connect up with my computer."

"This is part of your project?" Suddenly Ross wanted to know everything about this fascinating woman. "You mentioned a history."

"Yes. I teach computer science at Tech, but I've had this pet project I've been working on for years. The recent history of the field, the stuff that's going on right now in the industry. If it's not documented, important facts will be lost." As she spoke, the phone rang once before transferring the call through a modem in Gloria's office. "I receive data from all over the country. Then I have to sort through it and decide if it's worth incorporating in the text I'm compiling."

"It sounds like a lot of work."

"Yes. There's not room for much else in my life. I love it." This time it was her eyes that sparkled.

Ross regarded her for a long silent moment. He understood completely how she felt about her work. It was something they had in common. Looking into her intelligent brown eyes, he sensed there was a lot more they had in common. But she had her life and he had his. Like oil and water, they were not meant to mix. He took a step away from her, and asked quietly, "How's the ankle, Dr. Russell?"

Gloria sensed the moment he withdrew. She looked down at her bare foot. "Better. Much better, thank you, Major Adams." Like him, she took refuge in formality.

The sound of tires on gravel filled the suddenly awkward silence in the room.

"That'll be my buddies," Ross said. Zipping his jacket, he went to the door. "Thanks for taking time out of your busy schedule, Professor." He came to sharp attention and tossed her a jaunty salute. "See you around." Then he was gone.

"See you around, Major." Gloria's words echoed in the large kitchen. It had never seemed so empty. Thoughtfully, she sat down at the table and sipped her tea.

Chapter Three

Her encounter with Major Ross Adams had taken time out of her working day, Gloria realized as a dull ache rumbled through her stomach. It was well past three o'clock, and she had not yet eaten lunch. In short order, she cut several slices of her mother's homemade bread. Next came peanut butter and a layer of raspberry preserve. Carrying the sandwich and a mug of tea, she headed to her den and the work awaiting her.

Settling herself in front of the computer screen, she searched the menu of the disk already in the drive. Finding the new material, she displayed it on the screen and scrolled slowly through the data.

A movement outside the window caught her attention. Taking a bite of her sandwich, she swung her chair ninety degrees. Elbows propped on the desk top, Gloria watched as a brown, late-model pickup drove toward the hangar. Hitched behind the truck was a small trailer carrying what looked like a miniature fuel tank. Stenciled on the side were the words Aviation Fuel. The driver backed the trailer beside the hangar.

Ross Adams hopped out of the driver's seat and proceeded to uncouple the trailer. His task completed, he joined the other two men who emerged from the passenger's side. The three entered the hangar. Their excitement with the Stearman was obvious even from a distance. Sipping her tea absently, Gloria watched Ross unload a duffel bag from a storage compartment. He tossed it to one of his friends who hefted it onto his shoulders.

After the three emerged from the hangar, Ross secured the sliding doors. Realizing that she was being nosy, Gloria pushed away from the desk and faced her computer. As she scrutinized the data on the screen, she heard the truck pull up outside the house. Laughing voices filled the mudroom. In the next minute, heavy footsteps shook the staircase, then crisscrossed the floor above her head. From the sound of it, Ross and his buddies were getting a head start on moving into the apartment. The racket made it difficult to focus her attention on the screen.

The heavy whir of a vacuum cleaner started up. Gritting her teeth, Gloria pressed on with her work, trying to block out the noise. Ten interminable minutes later a loud knocking at the kitchen door broke what was left of Gloria's concentration.

Powering the computer down, she headed toward the kitchen door. If it was the major nuisance again, she'd tell him a thing or two—

"Margie!"

"Don't look so disappointed," her sister remarked as she breezed into the kitchen.

Gloria ignored the comment. "I've been trying to get you on the phone."

"That would be impossible the way things are going today." Margie tossed her handbag on the kitchen table.

"I take it business is booming. Sit down and I'll fix you a cup of tea."

"No tea for me, thanks. Aren't you working?"

"I was, but as you can imagine—" Gloria looked pointedly to the ceiling "—it hasn't been easy." The noise of the vacuum had given way to a scuffing noise that alternated with the clomping of booted feet. "Oh, and before I forget—" she reached into the pocket of her jeans "—here's a check for the first and last month's rent, plus a damage deposit."

Margie eagerly accepted the piece of paper. "This Major Ross Adams from Tampa, Florida, is a gift from heaven!" she declared as she scrutinized the check. Pleased, she looked at her sister. "What did he think about the apartment?"

"In his words, 'It will do.'" Gloria ran a hand through her hair. "He said he needs furniture, so I told him there was plenty to choose from up in the old loft."

"Good thinking!"

"Well, it's about time you rented the place out," was Gloria's reply.

"Yeah, but guys looking for a hangar don't grow on trees." Margie grinned. "Things are finally looking up for me."

Gloria sank into the chair opposite her sister. She took Margie's hand and gave it a squeeze. "That's wonderful. I don't know how you've managed, Margie. With a mortgage to pay and two kids to raise, not to mention getting a new business off the ground, I often wonder how you keep going."

"I keep going because I don't have any choice," Margie replied matter-of-factly. "I gave up long ago on the hope that Lon Carter was going to come back and take care of me and the kids again. And now that I know I can take care of myself, I don't want him back. Besides, I'm having too much fun playing the field." An impish grin curved her lips. "By marrying too young, I missed out on a lot. I'm making up for lost time."

"You're incorrigible!" Gloria scolded.

"Tell me something I don't know." Margie's eyes, so like Gloria's, danced with humor.

"Okay. The major up there wants to move in tomorrow, so we need to get that furniture out of the loft."

"Spoilsport. But you're right." Margie pulled a mirrored compact from her purse and proceeded to touch up her lipstick. "I have a date with Tony Bauman tonight. I'll get him to come over in the morning—"

"Tony Bauman! Of Mr. Muscle fame?"

"Uh-huh. We're celebrating tonight. I found him a new building for his health spa. Tony's business is booming, too, and he's outgrown his old place."

"You'd better watch out around Tony, Margie."

"Why do you say that?" Margie snapped the compact shut and turned her attention to her younger sister.

Gloria shrugged. "Well, I've heard about him."

"Yes?"

"He's got a reputation." Her sister sat very still, waiting patiently for her to continue. "A reputation as a . . . a philanderer, Margie!" Gloria frowned.

Her sister just laughed out loud. "What a nice, old-fashioned word!"

"It may be old-fashioned, but it fits."

"Don't look so worried, Gloria. I'm just going to dinner with the guy."

"That's a relief!"

Margie darted Gloria a sharp look. "Gloria, I sometimes think that my bad experience with marriage affected you more than it did me."

"I did learn a lot."

"I see. My marriage has turned you off the subject."

"Not exactly. I still believe in marriage," Gloria admitted. "But there are too many other things to do before I start thinking about settling down."

"What about you and Erik?" Margie asked. "I thought you and he were a hot item."

Gloria's eyes widened. "A hot item?" Her voice was incredulous. "Where did you hear that?"

"Oh, Blacksburg is a small town, remember? You can't hide a thing."

Indignant, Gloria sat up very straight. "I don't have anything to hide!"

Her sister's face fell. "That's too bad." Elbows on the table, she leaned forward. "Come on, you can tell me. Has he spent the night yet?"

Gloria couldn't believe her ears. "Of course not! He and I have never—" She did not go on.

Margie sank back into her chair. "That's too bad. At the rate you're going, you'll still be a virgin when you turn thirty."

"And what would be wrong with that?" Gloria retorted hotly.

A satisfied expression crossed Margie's face. "So you still are a—"

"You tricked me!"

Margie's lips twitched. "Yeah." She ducked her head modestly but was unable to suppress her smile.

Gloria stared at her older sister. "You're still as devious as you were when we were growing up."

"Flattery." Margie laughed. "I love it." And in the next moment the two women were laughing together. Margie turned serious first.

"Tell me, Gloria. What are you waiting for? Where men are concerned, I mean."

"The right time. There's no place for a man in my life, not just yet. If this project works out right, I'll be recognized as a leading authority in my field. It will probably get me tenure at the university, and that means job security. After that I can start looking for the right man."

"Sounds like the plans I had before Lon Carter came on the scene. Not that I'm complaining. He gave me two kids I'd never want to trade." Margie studied her sister. "Back to this right-man stuff. Will Erik Windom be in the running?"

"I don't know." Gloria shrugged. "Time will tell, I suppose."

This time Margie was not flippant. Instead, she sighed. "It always does, sooner or later." Narrowing her eyes, she asked, "What happens if the right time for you is the wrong time for Mr. Right?"

"Then I'd have to change the master plan."

"That sounds like the story of my life." She glanced at the clock on the kitchen wall. "Hey, I've got to go. Tony's waiting." She stood up. "Thanks for taking the time to show the apartment, Gloria. I'll be over tomorrow to sort through the furniture in the loft."

Gloria followed Margie out to the mudroom. Both women glanced toward the upstairs landing.

"All's quiet on the western front," Gloria murmured.

"What's that supposed to mean?"

"Oh, nothing. Just that the major and his noisy gang are gone." She avoided her sister's curious look. "And it's getting dark."

"It usually does this time of the day. That's why it's called night."

"Smart aleck!" Gloria reached out and gave her sister a quick hug. "Listen, be careful tonight. Don't do anything I wouldn't do."

"Then I'd better head for the nearest nunnery!" Margie's eyes danced as she stepped outside. Gloria stood in the doorway and waved goodbye. A light snow was falling, and a cold wind whistled around a dark corner.

As the taillights of Margie's sedan faded from sight, Gloria turned to go in. A softness brushed against her bare leg. She jumped.

"Where did you come from?" she demanded, peering down at a black cat that materialized out of the inky night.

"Meow."

She could tell that the animal was cold. "My sentiments exactly." Gloria bent and cautiously picked up the newcomer, turning toward the light for a better look. "I haven't seen you around here before." Yellow eyes blinked at her. "Let me see that collar." The medallion hanging from the animal's neck had an inscription.

Gloria read it out loud. "My name is Jane. I belong to . . . R. Adams!" It gave an address in Florida. "No wonder you're cold, Jane." Hugging the animal, she retreated to the warmth of the mudroom.

"He left you out in the cold, did he?" Gloria's voice was soft and soothing. "The cad. I know, it's another one of those old-fashioned words. But it fits so well."

Jane purred a response deep in her throat. "I'll bet you're hungry. I could rustle up some evaporated milk. Maybe even some tuna." Jane's ears pricked upright and Gloria laughed. She'd always loved cats.

In the warmth of the kitchen, she set the animal on the floor. Rummaging through her neat cupboards, Gloria darted a curious look at Jane. "Imagine leaving a beautiful girl like you out in the cold. Tomorrow, Jane, I'm going to give the major a piece of my mind." Jane's eyes closed in contentment and Gloria knew she had found a soul mate.

Every other Friday, Gloria met with the five graduate students who taught classes under her supervision. When she let Jane out for a morning run, there was no sign of Ross Adams. Her appointment on campus was set for nine, so there was no time to linger. After a quick shower, she stepped into a black lacy camisole and a matching pair of bikini panties. Searching through her closet, she pulled out one of her most becoming outfits, a black-and-white linen suit. Its slim skirt and bolero jacket accentuated her svelte figure. A yellow silk scarf tied in a bow to one side of her chin added flair. Suede heels and a matching black handbag completed the stylish outfit. Grabbing her winter coat, she locked the door behind her. Still no sign of the major, and Jane was nowhere in sight.

A light powdering of snow remained on the streets, but the sun shone brightly as Gloria pulled into a parking space overlooking the parade field. Burruss Hall loomed majestically over the center of the campus. Gloria stood quietly for a long moment, savoring the sights and sounds of Virginia Tech.

Anticipation always ran high at the beginning of each quarter, and with classes starting the following Monday, there was a definite excitement in the air.

A group of noisy cadets made their way along the sidewalk. Young and impressionable, they looked very handsome in the gray wool uniforms that always reminded Gloria of the Confederate Army. Indeed, many of the buildings that bordered the parade ground dated back to the 1860s. The old and new blended easily, and now, over a hundred years later, the university was the largest in the state of Virginia.

Gloria knew practically every building inside and out. There was a solidity, a timelessness to the place that appealed to her. She could count on one year on campus being much like the next, the only difference being a new set of faces in her classes. Gloria liked the even tenor of university life. Oh, there were small highs and some lows, but for the most part, it was smooth sailing. Filled with a sense of satisfaction, she headed for her office where the graduate students were waiting.

Two hours later the group broke up. They'd gone over the curriculum for the next quarter and discussed several problems left over from the previous grading period. After filling her department head in on her progress, Gloria decided to pick up some groceries on the way home.

Pulling into the driveway just after noon, she saw Ross's truck backed up to the hangar door. Music and laughter came from the inside of the building. Curious, Gloria left her groceries on the back steps and walked toward the sounds.

The sight of Margie dancing an energetic Charleston stopped Gloria dead in her tracks. Margie's partner was equally enthusiastic. But then, Ross Adams was that kind of man. He would never do anything halfway.

The music, high and squeaky, was coming from an ancient Victrola, complete with crank and sound horn. As the music faded, applause came from the loft where two pair of legs dangled over the edge. Gloria recognized one of the two men as Tony Bauman. He and a man in a blue air force uniform applauded. Margie curtsied to Ross, who gave her an equally elegant bow from the waist.

Gloria joined in the applause. "Bravo!" she called out.

Margie whirled around. "Gloria, hi!"

"Dr. Russell," Ross said, acknowledging her presence with a pleased smile.

"I was wondering where you'd gone to," her sister added, smoothing her skirt back into place.

"I had a meeting on campus this morning."

The two men descended from the loft, each of them carrying a small piece of furniture. Ross spoke up. "I'd like you to meet a friend of mine, Dr. Russell. This is Richard Stanek, and you probably know Tony Bauman."

Gloria extended her hand to the man in uniform. "Captain Stanek, I believe we talked on the phone yesterday."

"Yes, nice to meet you."

"Tony, how are you?" Gloria turned to Margie's friend. He reminded her a little bit of Lon Carter and that troubled her.

"Never better."

Margie spoke up. "We're helping Ross pick out furniture for his apartment." She waved a hand at the assortment of wood pieces scattered about the floor.

"Looks like there's enough here to furnish several apartments," Gloria noted.

"Yes," Margie agreed. "After Ross takes what he needs, I might have an auction. Some of these things are really valuable."

"Need any help?" Gloria volunteered.

Margie opened her mouth, but before she could reply, Ross stepped in. "No." He smiled. "We're almost finished."

"We were just getting ready to polish up some of these pieces," Margie explained. "If you change clothes, maybe you could—"

Again Ross interrupted. "I wouldn't dream of asking the professor to help."

"Gloria won't mind."

"I'm sure she wouldn't, Margie, but Dr. Russell and I have what could be termed a gentleman's agreement."

Margie looked from Ross to her sister. "Really?"

"The major's right," Gloria admitted, squelching the unusual feeling of being left out. "He knows I have important work to do." Out of the corner of her eye, she caught sight of Jane curled up in a pile of hay. "But while I'm here, Major, I'd like to discuss Jane with you."

At the sound of her name, the cat got up and stretched, then sauntered over to Gloria and rubbed against her new friend's leg. Gloria bent to pat the animal's head.

"You've met?" Ross seemed surprised.

"Yes." Gloria lifted her head. "We got acquainted last night, after you left her out in the snow." Her look was decidedly accusing. "She might have frozen to death!"

Ross bent to pick up his pet. Jane tucked her head under his chin and purred loudly as Ross caressed the thick black fur. "Jane's an outdoor cat."

"But surely she's not used to this kind of cold!"

He shrugged away her protests. "Cats are resourceful critters." His hand was gentle on Jane's head. "I don't worry about her, and she doesn't worry about me. That's why we get along so well. She seems to like you," Ross noted.

"I like her."

"I hope she wasn't any trouble."

"None at all. She's welcome anytime."

"Now you're making me jealous." A roguish grin accompanied his comment. Gloria felt her pulse start to race.

"I hope it was okay to give her some tuna." Aware that the other three were listening to their conversation, Gloria tried to keep the conversation strictly impersonal.

"It was fine, and thank you. Just a word of advice." He put the cat down. Jane immediately went back to rubbing against Gloria's ankle. "Jane is very loyal to the people she likes and she tends to show her appreciation. Any day now, she'll be bringing you your very own field mouse or snake."

"Really?"

"Yes." There was a note of concern in his voice.

"Well, I guess I'd better not get too friendly with Jane."

"No, it wouldn't be a good idea to get too friendly." They were both aware that her relationship with the cat was not the real topic of conversation.

It made her remember that they were not alone. "Well, I'd better be going. I have work to do. Nice meeting you." She waved to Stek and Tony and ignored her sister's look of curiosity.

Back at the house, she changed clothes, hanging the suit in the closet and tossing the lingerie into the clothes hamper. Comfortable in jeans and sweater, she unpacked her groceries. Occasional bursts of laughter from the hangar made her feel the odd man out. Chiding herself for being foolish, she headed for her computer terminal.

Standing in the center of the office, she surveyed its contents—the bookcase with years of texts placed neatly side by side—the desk with its clutter of notes and stacks of printouts. Victrola music filtered through the closed window. For the first time in months, she did not feel like working. But she had a schedule to adhere to. With a sigh of frustration, she booted her system and forced herself to concentrate.

A few hours later, Margie popped her head through the office doorway. "We're all done. Ross is moved in."

Gloria looked up from the computer screen. "That's nice."

"He's nice."

"Yes."

Margie tilted her head and observed her sister. She opened her mouth as if to say something, then changed her mind. "See you at Mother and Dad's on Sunday."

Saturday dawned bright and distinctly warmer than the previous day. Spring was definitely on the way. When Gloria went out to get the paper, she saw Ross in the hangar, working on the Stearman's engine. He waved, and Gloria waved back.

She lingered over breakfast. Standing in front of the kitchen window, she washed the small amount of dishes from her meal and watched Ross work on the aircraft. He seemed totally involved in the project. After she'd put away the last plate, Gloria set about washing several loads of laundry, vacuuming the carpets and dusting the furniture between cycles. Moving the last small load of clothes from the washer to the dryer, she decided she was in the mood to edit the previous day's work before getting ready for her date with Erik.

At five, after an afternoon's successful work, Gloria dressed for her date. The simple white wool dress contrasted beautifully with her coal-black hair. A touch of pink lip gloss and a spray of cologne were her only accessories. Erik Windom arrived promptly at six o'clock. With a smile, he kissed Gloria on the cheek. As always, he told her that she looked lovely, and as always, she politely thanked him.

Escorting her to his car, Erik noted the lights in the hangar. A clanging sound rang from behind the closed doors.

"What's that noise?" Erik enquired.

"Oh, that. It's Margie's new tenant. He's doing some engine work."

Her answer satisfied Erik, and climbing into the driver's seat, he asked about her project.

After a pleasant dinner at a restaurant just off campus, Erik drove them to the student center.

"They're starting a series of Errol Flynn movies," he told Gloria as they walked up the steps of Squires Student Center.

"Perfect!" She and Erik shared a love for old Hollywood swashbucklers. Evenings out with Erik were never a surprise, but his stability was what appealed to her. He was a perfect gentleman, reserved, articulate and unfailingly polite. And he never pressed her for anything more than companionship.

They stopped in front of the theater doors. "*The Dawn Patrol,*" Erik read. "One of my all-time favorites! You'll love it."

They found seats and settled in for the show. Five minutes into the movie, a remake of an early Howard Hughes film, Gloria started to fidget.

"Are you all right?" Erik leaned close to her in the dark.

"Yes, I'm fine." But she wasn't, she realized as he turned his attention back to the film. The hero in the movie was an aviator, flying over France in a biplane during World War I. Despite Flynn's dark hair, he reminded her vividly of Ross Adams. He was dashing. Daring. A maverick. A man committed to flying. And he died in the end.

White-knuckled, Gloria watched the credits fill the screen.

"That was great!" Erik exclaimed as the lights came up. "They used actual footage from the war." When Gloria did not answer, he turned to her in concern. "What's the matter? Didn't you like it?"

Her mouth was dry, and she swallowed. "I'm not sure," she replied truthfully. "It was pretty grim, all those planes crashing."

"It was based on the truth, Gloria. In real life, the ending is not always a happy one." Erik assisted her to her feet and held her coat. "I can tell you one thing, though. As fascinating as those planes are, you couldn't pay me to fly in one of those things."

"I wonder..." Erik did not hear her.

They drove straight home. A full moon rode high in the sky, and as Erik walked her to the kitchen door, Gloria did not bother with a light.

"Would you like to come in for coffee?" she offered, inserting her key in the lock.

"No, thanks, it's late."

Gloria turned back to him. "I enjoyed tonight."

"You seemed a little subdued," was his response.

"It was the movie."

Erik smiled down at her. "You're a sweet girl." And he bent to kiss her. His mouth on hers was chaste, a friendly brushing of lips.

A loud crash made them jump apart. Gloria dashed for the light switch. On the second-floor landing, Ross Adams was hopping around on one foot.

"What do you think you're doing up there?" she demanded.

"I stubbed my toe!"

"I mean what are you doing up there in the dark!"

"I was looking for a light switch!"

"Major Adams!"

"All right! I wanted to talk to you about something, but I think under the circumstances, it can wait." Ross looked pointedly at Erik.

Gloria sighed. "Since you went to all that trouble, what is it?"

"No, no. You've got company."

"Oh, Erik, excuse me. This is Ross Adams, my new neighbor. Major Adams, this is Erik Windom."

Erik stepped forward, hand outstretched. Ross met him at the foot of the stairs. "Oh, sorry." Ross transferred a wad of material from his right hand to the left. The men shook hands.

"So, Major, what's on your mind?" Gloria persisted.

Ross waved her question aside. "Tomorrow is soon enough, Dr. Russell."

"I won't be here tomorrow." She waited, not bothering to disguise her impatience.

Ross looked from Gloria to Erik. "It's all right," Gloria said. "Erik is a good friend. We don't have any secrets."

"But this is a private..."

"Good grief, Major Adams. I don't have all night!" Gloria snapped at him.

Ross rolled his eyes and sighed. "Okay. I just wanted to return these." He opened his left hand and held up her black camisole and bikini panties.

Gloria gasped. "Where did you get those?"

Behind her, Erik coughed. "I think the major is right. This is a private matter. Good night, Gloria." He made a hasty retreat to the door.

"But—"

"Some other time, Gloria." And he was gone.

The silence in the room was deafening. Gloria turned. Now she knew what it felt like to have one's blood boil. Very slowly she closed the distance between her and Ross. He held her undergarments in front of him, as if the delicate fabric would protect him from her obvious fury.

"You did that on purpose," she said, drawing the words out very slowly.

Ross backed up the stairs. "I tried to tell you..."

Brown eyes blazed hotly. "Where did you get my underwear?"

"I was getting to that."

Her glare told him to get to the point.

"You left them in the dryer. I folded them for you."

Gloria kept moving toward him. Ross backed farther up the stairs. "You deliberately let Erik get the wrong idea." They were on the landing halfway up to his apartment.

The expression on his face was all innocence. "Why would I want to do something like that?"

Gloria stopped. "Oh, there's no talking to you!" And she stepped away from him.

"Watch out!"

She felt Jane's tail beneath her feet the same instant the cat let out a howl of pain. Gloria jerked forward, the movement propelling her straight into Ross's arms. Looking up, she found her face very close to his.

Ross stared down at Gloria, a question burning in his eyes. "Does your boyfriend always kiss you like that?" His voice was low and husky.

"Yes, not that it's any of—"

It all happened too fast for her to resist. His mouth covered hers. The kiss was like him: unorthodox, demanding, unsettling. Unique.

But too short.

Ross pulled his lips from hers. "Now you've been properly kissed." His eyes blazed with emotion. "And if you think I'm going to apologize, you're crazy!"

Shocked at her own heady reaction to the kiss, Gloria reached out and grabbed her lingerie still entangled in Ross's fingers.

"I'm going to take these and go back down the stairs. You—" she pointed an accusing finger at him "—are going to go back into your apartment. And the next time we see each other, we'll pretend that this never happened." She was breathing hard.

Ross sighed, thrusting agitated fingers through his hair. "Look. I don't know why I did that."

"It doesn't matter."

"But it does! It seems like every time I get around you, I do something stupid." One foot moved.

"Don't come any closer!"

He didn't. "Gloria. I'd like to pretend this never happened, but in all honesty, I don't think I can."

"Yes, you can, Ross." Panic surged through her, and she did not realize that this was the first time she'd used his first name. "You can do anything you set your mind to!"

Gloria turned and fled down the stairs and into her apartment, closing the kitchen door firmly behind her. "*I* can do anything I set my mind to." With clenched fists, she made her way into her den and turned on her computer. There she felt safe and peaceful, insulated from a turbulent world filled with people who had the power to rock her boat. Not people, she amended. *Person*. One man whose kiss had awakened a part of her that she had not known existed.

Chapter Four

Just as she was sitting down to plunge into her work Monday morning, Gloria was interrupted by the chime of bells from the rarely used front door. In the day and a half that had passed since Ross Adams had kissed her, she had been moderately successful in keeping thoughts of the man at bay. Wondering what she would say to him, she hurried to the door.

It wasn't Ross. It was a cheery, freckle-faced teenager named Kathy delivering a box of dishes for Ross to use in his new kitchen. The girl's father, Gloria learned, was Ross's commanding officer at the ROTC unit on campus. When Kathy discovered that Gloria was a professor at the university, she eagerly asked for advice on curriculum. The vivacious girl would be entering Tech as a freshman the following August. It was an hour before Kathy ran out of questions.

Gloria hurried back to her office only to hear the doorbell chime once more. Wondering if the girl had forgotten something, Gloria dashed back and pulled the squeaky door quickly open.

An older, attractive woman in her mid-twenties juggled a paper bag and a sleepy baby in her arms.

"I'm Harriet Stanek. Is this where Ross Adams lives?"

"His place is upstairs, actually," Gloria explained. "But he's at work."

"Oh, I know. I was just wondering if I could drop off this bag of pots and pans." The baby squirmed in his mother's arms, and Gloria caught the sack just as it slid out of Harriet's arms.

"Thanks." Harriet breathed a sigh of relief. "I haven't quite got the hang of carrying two things at a time, especially when one of them is a ball of energy."

"I can put these in the mudroom where the major will see them when he comes in." The baby's wail forced Gloria to raise her voice in midsentence.

"He's thirsty," Harriet apologized, "and his bottle of juice is empty."

"I have some apple juice in the fridge, if you'd like a refill."

"Would I!" The young mother followed Gloria into the kitchen. "I can't think straight, not to mention drive safely, with him crying in his car seat."

"I'll just put this sack out here." Gloria opened the kitchen door to the mudroom. "Help yourself to the juice. Top shelf in the fridge."

When Gloria returned, Harriet was handing the bottle to the eager baby, who immediately quieted down. "I couldn't help but notice the computer printouts," Harriet remarked, nodding in the direction of some papers Gloria had left on the kitchen table. "I used to be a programmer until the baby came along."

"Are you planning on going back to work?" Gloria asked, realizing the woman was eager for some adult conversation. Harriet ended up staying for coffee while the two women discussed different aspects of their careers. After a second refill of apple juice for the baby, Harriet was on her way, leaving an invitation for Gloria to visit Harriet when she was in town.

Dismayed at the way time had slipped away, Gloria hurried back to her office, vowing to ignore the doorbell for the next four hours at least.

A few hours later, just as she was tackling a particularly difficult section of data, a knock at the back door interrupted her concentration for a third time. She tried to ignore the sound, hoping that whoever was there would go away. He didn't and the knocking became louder. Sighing with frustration, Gloria made her way to the kitchen door.

"Boy, am I glad someone is here!" a young man of about seventeen exclaimed. "My mom would have me court-martialed if I brought this casserole back home with me!"

"Don't tell me," Gloria said in a resigned voice. "This is for Ross Adams, and you want me to keep it warm for his dinner." The major might have promised to stay out of her way, but she couldn't say the same for his army of friends.

"Would you? That would be great!" He thrust the dish and thermal pot holder into her hands and was off before she could discover his identity.

"Why me?" Gloria muttered to herself. Perhaps the air force had put an ad in the local paper: "Ross Adams in town. See Gloria Russell for details." Now she was stuck with watching for the major's arrival. She set the dish on the counter. The aroma wafting from beneath the glass lid was heavenly—and a painful reminder that she had not eaten all day. By the time she had her dinner going, she heard Ross's footsteps in the mudroom. Flinging open the kitchen door, casserole in hand, she caught him just as he was about to mount the stairs.

It was the first time she'd seen him in his air force uniform. He wore a bulky blue sweater with epaulets that sported a gold leaf on each broad shoulder. Beneath the V-neck was a light blue shirt and dark blue tie. Matching blue slacks tapered to shiny black leather shoes. Tucked in his webbed belt was a slender flight cap, its blue edged in silver. No man had a right to look that good in government issue. And Ross Adams looked better than good. He took her breath away.

"Your dinner, Major Adams." She held out the casserole. "And before you get the wrong idea, I didn't make it. I have trouble enough getting myself fed."

"Who brought it?" Ross's blue eyes were an exact match to his crisp military shirt.

"A tall, dark-haired boy who was not happy with the thought of returning home with the casserole undelivered."

"Sounds like the Sarge's kid." Ross retraced his steps and took the dish from Gloria. "Thanks."

"He wasn't the only one who dropped by." She did not hide her disgruntlement. "There are dishes in that box from Kathy and cooking utensils in the sack from Harriet." She motioned to the landing.

"Sounds like my friends have kept you busy, Doc." He acknowledged her tone of voice. "This casserole smells great. I worked straight through lunch and didn't even take time out for coffee."

"I wish I could say the same thing," Gloria muttered as he loped up the stairs, the clatter of his feet on the wood drowning out her comment. With another quick thanks Ross disappeared into his apartment.

So much for his vow never to forget the kiss they'd shared! Doc! He'd called her Doc! He was obviously more interested in his dinner than in her! Gloria flounced back into the kitchen and closed the door. The last thing on her mind was food. How could he act so blasé after what had happened between them? After all, that hadn't been an ordinary kiss.

It had been the most intense three seconds of her life.

Stop!

Closing the kitchen door behind her, she took a deep breath. She was a scientist, she reminded herself. As a scientist, she knew that there was always a logical explanation for a perplexing phenomenon. In this case, it was hormones. After all, she was twenty-six years old and had not had a lot of experience with men. This was bound to have happened to her sooner or later, this crazy reaction to a person of the opposite sex. What did she expect, she thought with frustration. She'd gone straight from the farm to the university. To say that she'd led a sheltered life was the understatement of the century. She was just the kind of girl who would swoon at the feet of a dashingly handsome fighter pilot. Gloria's hand went to her lips. She could still feel the imprint of his mouth on hers.

Anger surged through her. She'd do better to take care of her growling stomach instead of daydream about a man who probably had a girl in every airport. She fixed her plate and carried it into her office, hoping to make up for lost time.

Tuesday was a modified version of Monday, with various people stopping by and asking for Ross Adams. Wednesday, the daytime crowd ebbed, but during the evening hours, she was interrupted half a dozen times by people knocking at her door. Wearily Gloria directed them to the upstairs apartment.

By Thursday afternoon, Gloria's frustration was running high, and she was considering stenciling directions to the Adams apartment on the back door. As she was fixing herself a cup of camomile tea in the kitchen, she heard a scratching at her door.

"That does it—oh, it's you," she said, relieved at the sight of Jane sitting on the doorstep. "I thought for sure you'd be another card-carrying member of the Ross Adams Fan Club making sure he lacks for nothing while he's in Virginia." The black cat walked haughtily into the kitchen and ignored Gloria's comment. "You're still holding a grudge, are you?" Jane sat back on her haunches and proceeded to carefully groom her right front paw.

"You know that things can't go on like this," she informed Jane, who continued to ignore her. "Blackmail," Gloria mused. "I'll ply you with drink, and then you'll have to forgive me for mashing your tail." She produced a small can of evaporated milk from the cupboard. "After all, I didn't do it on purpose." From the corner of her eye, Gloria noted the cat's surreptitious glances.

The aloof feline pretended to devote her attention to cleaning her paws until the saucer of cream was placed squarely in front of her. With a regal nod of her dark head, the cat came to all fours and started to lap daintily at the treat.

Gloria leaned back against the kitchen counter and watched with amusement.

Finished with the milk, Jane turned her back on Gloria and loped quickly out of the room. She pushed the screen door open and slipped out into the yard. Gloria ran after her, holding the back door wide open. "Hey! Don't I even get a thank-you? Where'd you learn your manners? Oh, never mind! I keep forgetting who you belong to!"

She started to go back inside when Jane streaked back into the mudroom. Hands on her hips, Gloria stared at the cat, who had parked herself at the entrance to the kitchen. There was something in her mouth. Something small and dark. And fuzzy.

"Uh, Jane—"

The cat tossed her head in a very unfeline manner. The fuzzy creature flew out of the cat's mouth and skittered across the shiny kitchen floor. Jane darted after it.

Gloria ran to the kitchen door to see the cat paw at the tiny dark brown creature—a rodent. Gloria took one step away from the kitchen. It was too small and too dark to be a mouse. What else could it be? She remembered similarly furred animals darting in and out of the woodpile out back. Shrews!

"Jane, I will never forgive—" Gloria backed slowly toward the exit and bumped squarely into a broad chest.

"Hey!" Ross Adams exclaimed as she whirled around. "What's wrong?" He steadied her by the shoulders.

Panic showed clearly on her face. "It's a . . . a . . ." She drew in a deep breath, but could not prevent her voice from sounding like a squeak. "A shrew!"

"You? Never!"

"Not me! In there!" Irritation brought the return of her voice. "I gave Jane some milk and she went out and brought me a shrew! It's loose!" Her finger pointed dramatically to her kitchen.

Amusement changed to immediate concern on Ross's face. "Stay here." With a reassuring squeeze to her shoulders, he released her and went in search of his mischievous pet.

"You don't have to tell me twice," Gloria gasped. Trying to slow the pounding of her heart, she leaned weakly against the washing machine. Her reaction to the presence of a rodent was so disgustingly feminine, but it was a fear she'd never been able to conquer, despite having lived on a farm. One glimpse of a dark furry rodent and rationality vanished.

Ross appeared in front of her. "Was this what you were referring to?" He held up a round dark ball of fuzz.

Gloria edged away from him. "Yes!" she yelped.

His chuckle filled the air, then he squeezed the ball in his hand. It gave out a high-pitched sound.

Gloria gasped, then took a closer look. Ross squeezed the fuzz ball again, then tossed it to Jane who was prancing eagerly on her black feet. The brown ball bounced as it hit the floor and gave out a simultaneous squeak.

"It's a toy!" Gloria's tone of voice was accusing.

"A very realistic one, you have to admit." Ross was trying hard to hold back his mirth.

"Do I ever!" In the next moment, Gloria started laughing at the absurdity of her reaction to a fur-covered rubber mouse. "I should be angry. Or at the least embarrassed for letting that thing scare me."

"But you aren't." It was the voice of approval.

"No. I'm too relieved!" They smiled at each other, the atmosphere between them easy and relaxed.

Owing to a warming trend in the weather, he wore a summer-style uniform, which consisted of a short-sleeved blue shirt open at the neck. The dark blue slacks were neatly tailored. Again, his flight cap with its gold leaf, signifying his rank as a major, was tucked into his belt. It was a simple uniform, but on him it looked wonderful.

Ross broke into her thoughts. "This has been a tough week for you," he observed. "Adjusting to a new neighbor with a noisy airplane and noisier friends—not to mention a temperamental cat on the premises. All that and we're still friends."

Not a word she'd have used to describe their relationship up to that point, but she nodded nevertheless. Then she noted the boyish tilt to his blond head and that familiar glint in his blue eyes.

"Why do I get the feeling that that wasn't just another casual statement?"

"I can't hide anything from you, can I?" His lips quirked at the corners.

"Not anymore," Gloria shook her head. "I've got your number, remember?"

"Funny you should put it that way—"

"Go ahead," she sighed. "Spit it out."

"I can't get the phone company to come out for a couple of weeks. I gave your number to my office, just in case they need to get in contact with me after duty hours."

"After duty hours—" She had already noticed that military men had their own special jargon.

"Yup." He grinned. "Seven-thirty a.m. to 4:30 p.m., in civilian time. But a soldier is never really off duty. Hope you don't mind. If anyone calls for me, it will be official business only."

"Well, as a taxpayer, I guess I won't mind."

"I knew you'd be a good sport!" Then he turned on his heel. "See ya!" With one of his jaunty salutes, he took the stairs two at a time and disappeared into his apartment.

"Sure—see ya!" she mimicked to his closed door. Apparently what had happened between them the other night was history. He'd forgotten all about their kiss and now thought she was a good sport! Once more indignation rose in her chest.

Jane pranced up to her, toy in mouth, and presented it proudly to Gloria. With a grimace, she bent and took the mouse from the cat's mouth.

"You!" she held the fuzzy creature up by its rubber tail. "If I never see you again, it will be too soon!"

She marched to the back door and tossed the thing outside. Jane darted after it and started to bring it back to Gloria.

"Uh-uh," she said from the safety of the mudroom. "I'm going back to work!"

It was after midnight when Gloria jerked to a sitting position in her bed. A sharp noise had roused her suddenly from a deep, much-needed sleep. After the episode with Jane and her furry friend, she'd worked straight through the dinner hour and on into the evening. Groggily she listened carefully, straining her eyes in the dark room. Nothing. She fell back on to her pillow.

The sound penetrated her mind again. Gloria groaned as she recognized it to be the phone. She followed the strident sound into her office. "Hello." As she spoke, she bent to snap on the desk lamp.

"Dr. Russell?"

"Yes."

"This is Sergeant Powers speaking. Sorry to disturb you, but Major Ross Adams left this number in case of emergency. Is he there?"

"No, of course he's not here!" she snapped. "He lives upstairs!"

"Excuse me, ma'am, if this is an inconvenience, but this is a military recall. I need to get hold of the major. Would you mind..."

"Certainly!" Shame washed through her for being so abrupt with the man. He was only doing his job. "I'll get him for you." She dropped the phone and ran down the hallway, through the kitchen and up the stairs. She pounded on Ross Adams's door.

"Ross! It's me! Gloria! Open up! You're wanted on the phone!"

A light appeared in the transom and the door swung open. Knowing eyes swept over Gloria's slender figure, taking in the sheerness of her nightgown, her bare feet and charmingly mussed hair.

"Lady, you're a sight for sore eyes." His voice was husky from sleep. Like her, he had not bothered with a robe and wore nothing but a pair of white pajama bottoms that rode low on tanned hips and below a wide muscular chest.

Gloria gulped. "Well, put those eyes back in their sockets and get to the phone! It's an emergency—some sort of military crisis!" She turned on her heel, only too glad to get away from the light spilling out of his apartment. Light that had outlined the slenderness of her body beneath the fine cotton of her gown.

"I don't care if we've been invaded by Martians—" He followed her down the stairs.

"Don't get any ideas," she warned as she handed him the receiver from the wall phone in the kitchen.

"I was only enjoying the view. You wouldn't send a guy off to war without something to sustain him, would you?"

"Just answer the phone, Major!" she hissed, holding a hand over the mouthpiece.

"So heartless," he admonished softly but did as she asked. "Adams here."

He listened intently for a long moment, then nodded his head. "Will do." With his right hand, he clicked off the phone, then quickly dialed a number. "Stek, it's Ross. This is a telephone recall. You know what to do."

Gloria watched Ross closely. She was tense, wondering what the emergency was. When he hung up the receiver and leaned back against the wall, she could hold her curiosity no longer.

"Well—Stek might know what to do, but I don't."

Ross's smile was a lazy one. "You can go back to bed."

"That's easy for you to say! You're used to wars and crises. Do you really expect me to sleep while you go off to...to..." At a loss for words, she waved her hand impatiently.

"To my bed."

"But the recall! Doesn't that mean you have to report somewhere?"

He shook his head. "Not this time. That was a telephone recall. It's just a test to see if the system works."

"A test! They woke me up in the middle of the night for a test?"

"'Fraid so."

Gloria's eyes narrowed in suspicion. "You knew they'd do that, didn't you?" Hands went indignantly to her hips, and she advanced slowly but surely toward him.

"No, really." He edged around the table.

"Don't lie to me!"

"I wouldn't—"

"Wouldn't you?"

His steps took him toward the door. "I'm new at the detachment. I suspected they might call—"

"You suspected!"

"All right!" Standing in the doorway, he hitched up his pajama bottoms. "I hoped they'd call." And he crossed defiant arms across his bare chest. A chest that was lightly dusted with beautiful gold hair.

"Of all the..."

"Has anyone ever told you that you're beautiful when you're angry?"

"All the time!" she lied baldly.

"Oh." He managed to look crestfallen. "If the sergeant hadn't been able to reach me tonight, I'd be in hot water—"

"You're in hot water, anyway." She slammed the kitchen door in his face.

A light tapping came from the glass window. Gloria jerked the door open in exasperation. "What is it this time?"

"I just wanted to say thanks."

"That's it?" She looked for an ulterior motive, but when he merely nodded, she added, "You're welcome. I think." And she closed the door again. Through the glass, she heard his muffled voice.

"That was an authentic, official recall, Gloria."

"I know, I know." Wearily, she leaned her head back against the door.

"I'm going now."

"Good."

"I'm going upstairs."

"You said that already."

"I'm going upstairs to take a cold shower, Gloria."

"What?"

"I said—"

"I know what you said!"

"Cold, Gloria. Very cold."

"You do that, Ross." She fled down the hallway to her office and hung up the phone extension. Back in bed, she buried her head with a pillow.

The sound of running water kept her awake for what seemed like hours.

Chapter Five

Gloria was much too busy the next day to dwell on her late-night encounter with Ross Adams. It was Friday again, and she rushed to get to the campus. She shouldn't have rushed, she realized five minutes into her meeting with her graduate teachers. It seemed spring fever was epidemic.

The usual eager intelligent faces wore expressions of bemusement. Thoughts faltered in midsentence. Longing glances were directed toward the window with its view of blue skies and fluffy white clouds. A knock on Gloria's office door was welcomed by all.

"Come in," Gloria invited.

The door swung inward. It was Erik Windom. "Oh, I'm sorry—you're still in conference," he apologized. "I'll come back." He started to close the door again.

"No, no." Gloria stood up, noting the relief on the faces in the room. "We're all finished, aren't we?" A simultaneous exclamation of agreement was the most enthusiastic response of the morning. Like her students, Gloria quickly gathered up her papers.

"Are you done for the day?" Erik asked when they were alone.

"Yes, thank goodness." She stuffed her notes into her leather briefcase. "I'm on my way home."

"Then I'll walk you to your car."

"That would be nice." As they strode side by side down the stairs, they chatted about inconsequential things—the weather, the interest that outside companies were showing in the Blacksburg economy, a new restaurant opening on Main Street.

Outside in the brisk air, Erik accompanied Gloria to the curb. "Where's your car?"

"That way—"

He took her by the elbow and crossed the tree-lined street. "Looks like spring is about to burst open," Erik commented, looking up at the bud-covered trees.

Gloria darted her friend a curious look. It wasn't like Erik to muse over the advent of a season. He was like her—far too down-to-earth. It was obvious there was something else on his mind and he was having difficulty broaching the subject.

She opened her car door and tossed her briefcase across the seat. Instead of getting in, she closed the door and leaned back against it. "Erik, I've been meaning to talk to you about what happened the other night—"

A flush of red up his neck told her she'd correctly guessed what had been bothering him.

"It wasn't what it looked like, you know," she went on. "I barely know the man—"

Erik placed a hand on her arm. "I know that, Gloria! And I know you too well to get the wrong idea." His eyes were apologetic. "I just felt bad about leaving you there alone with him. I should have changed my mind and stayed for that coffee, but— Well, I guess I'm not good at confrontations. I wouldn't blame you if you were angry with me."

"Angry? With you?" A rush of warmth for her friend engulfed her. Impulsively she leaned toward him and pressed a quick friendly kiss on one corner of his lips. "Never!"

Pleasure filled his eyes, and he straightened to his full height. "Good. And you won't take it wrong when I tell you I won't be seeing you this Saturday? I'm flying to Richmond this afternoon for a math seminar."

"I won't take it wrong at all, Erik! That's the seminar you've been talking about for months, isn't it?"

"Yes. I'm the featured speaker." Quiet pride lit his eyes.

"That's wonderful!"

"Thanks. I'd better get going. I have to pack and get to the airport."

"Need a ride?"

"No. A bunch of us from the department are going together." He took her hand and gave it a parting squeeze before darting across the street to his car.

"Erik," Gloria called out, raising her hand in a wave. "Knock 'em dead!"

His laugh was mildly triumphant. "I'll do my best!" She watched him back his tiny sports car into the street. It was the same car he'd owned since graduate school. With a roar, it disappeared into the noonday traffic.

Slipping into her own vehicle, Gloria rolled down the windows, then joined the flow of automobiles circling the parade field. As she came even with Burruss Hall, a crowd of students swarmed into the crosswalk. Enjoying the fresh warmth of the air, Gloria was content to wait for the pedestrians.

The rhythmic sound of marching feet caught her attention. The Corps of Cadets was out in full force, practicing drills on the grassy grounds. A dozen squadrons of fresh-faced, gray-clad cadets marched in precise military formation. A student commander sang out orders for the drill. On the sidelines, people of all ages stopped to admire the precision movements of the uniformed young men and women. Gloria was no exception.

There was something heart stopping about watching a military parade, the flags flying, drums rolling. Brass glittered beneath the spring sun. The sight conjured pride and patriotism, and despite the fact that the cadets practiced on the drill field almost daily, Gloria was never left unaffected. They were the young men and women of the country's future. It was they who would voluntarily defend the American way of life, if that need should ever arise. Her eyes shifted to the monument towering over the tiny chapel at the east end of the field. Above the place of worship rose the war memorial, a visible reminder of the numbers of Virginia Tech cadets who had given their lives in service to their country. Eight limestone pylons represented Brotherhood, Honor, Leadership, Sacrifice,

Service, Loyalty, Duty and *Ut Prosim*, the University's motto, That I May Serve.

A movement on the parade ground caught Gloria's attention. A formation of military men stood at attention, the blue uniforms of the air force standing out in sharp contrast to the olive tones of their army counterparts. Gloria had no trouble recognizing Ross Adams, his gold-flecked hair not completely hidden by the silver-edged flight cap. He was standing at attention, his back proudly straight, his shoulders held rigid.

As the first squadron of cadets marched past the reviewing group, Ross and his fellow officers brought their right hands up in salute to the flag. The student commander looked smartly in their direction, his sabre flashing a silver tribute. The young voice barked out orders to the squadron.

Behind Gloria, a car horn beeped. One glance in the rearview mirror told her that she'd been so involved in watching the movements on the parade ground that she'd been holding up traffic. Hurriedly she pressed on the accelerator. Thank goodness the major had not seen her blocking traffic, practically swooning over the sight of him in his dashing dress blues!

Gloria drove home to find a stack of mail waiting. Sorting through it, she was pleased to note several thick envelopes, one from a contact in the Silicon Valley and another from a colleague in Japan. Her work would be incomplete if she ignored the development of electronics in other industrialized countries. Eager to peruse the information, she hurried to her desk.

* * *

Saturday morning found Gloria striding energetically through the woods beyond the farmhouse. The air was filled with the illusive scent of unfolding foliage. Adjusting her headphones over her bare head, Gloria listened to another tape she'd received from the MIT professor. It had been accompanied by a stack of documents that she'd designated as her afternoon project.

Nearing the grass runway, Gloria snapped off the tape and listened for the now-familiar sound of the Stearman. Nothing. Glancing up and down the airstrip, she did not see the plane. Feeling safe, she strode across the expanse of grass. The door to the hangar, she noted, was closed. Against her will, she took a detour past the wooden building and peeked through a dusty windowpane. The Stearman was gone, which meant that the Red Baron was not on the premises.

She couldn't get the man out of her mind. She attributed that to Ross's forceful personality. His ability to stand out in a room was a trait she'd noticed almost right off. He was a man who would attract attention in a crowd of thousands. And not just because of his good looks. With those keen, intelligent eyes and that aura of command, he was an exceptional man. A man who got what he wanted. And he'd made no secret about wanting her. The disturbing thing about it all was the undeniable fact that Gloria was equally attracted to him.

It puzzled her, that sizzling awareness of him as a man. They were complete opposites: he the Red Baron, a daredevil who soared to the sun; and she—well, she was earthbound, her nose invariably buried in the pages of a book or glued to a computer screen. She lived by theorems and rules. He went his own way, defying the rules, tempting the fates every day of the week. Gloria did not want to tempt the fates. She wanted a sure thing. The two of them had absolutely nothing in common.

Except one quick kiss. She had only to close her eyes, and the memory of that moment would wash over her. She experienced once again the heat of his breath on her cool skin, the delicious tingle of his lips touching hers, the sensuality of his hard mouth pressing firmly over hers. Then came the weak knees and speeding pulse. After that a dizzying breathlessness.

Remembering where she was, Gloria forced her eyes open to the here and now. She was no teenager to daydream over a guy who looked delicious in air force blues. She was a woman with work to do. Taking a deep, calming breath, she hurried across the yard toward the house. Halfway there, the sound of a car pulling into the driveway caught her attention.

"Dad!"

Barry Russell stepped out of his old pickup parked behind Ross's newer model. Tall and ruddy, Gloria's father had the same dark hair as his two daughters. Streaks of gray gave him a grandfatherly air, but his physical condition was that of a much younger man.

"Nice," her father commented as he strode past the vehicle.

"What brings you this way?" Gloria asked.

"Margie ordered paint for the major's living room. Your mother baked some cookies for you, so I volunteered to bring both things over." He handed her a foil-wrapped plate, still warm on the bottom. "Is he in?"

"No." She caught the flash of disappointment in her father's eyes. "His truck is here, but the plane is gone. There's no telling when he'll be back."

"Too bad." Carrying the can of paint, Barry followed Gloria into the house. "I wanted to see the Stearman. Oh, well, I'll just put the paint on the steps so he'll see it."

"How about a cup of coffee?"

"Sounds good. Maybe the major will arrive while I wait."

As her father took a seat at the kitchen table, Gloria realized how his life had changed since he'd sold the farm. He obviously had a surfeit of time on his hands and not a great deal of excitement in his life. Hence the eagerness to see Ross Adams's plane.

Knowing her father would not appreciate instant coffee, she filled the glass carafe of the coffee maker with water. After she poured the liquid into the tank, she pulled out a small canister of coffee and neatly measured out the grains. While the coffee dripped, she unwrapped the cookies and set them in the center of the table.

She sat down opposite her father. "What have you been doing lately, Dad?" She munched on a cookie.

"Nothing."

"What?"

"I said nothing. Absolutely nothing." He leaned back in the chair and crossed his arms over his chest. "How about you?"

"Oh!" The quick change of subject disconcerted her. "I'm in the middle of my project. Same old stuff, too much paperwork."

"But you enjoy it." It was a gruff statement.

"Yes."

"Good."

Noting that the coffee was done, she went to pour them each a cup. As she carried the mugs to the table, she studied her father's face. "You're not happy, are you, Dad?"

Her statement caught him off guard. "I'm happy about a lot of things. You and Margie and your brothers make me happy. You've all become successful in your own fields. Margie's kids make me happy. Your mother makes me happy." He took a gulp of hot coffee.

"That's not what I'm talking about."

He rubbed a hand over his face. "I know." Gloria was well aware that her father was not used to putting his emotions into words. "Damn, but I'm not good at doing nothing!" He stood up and started to pace back and forth across the kitchen. "You're not exactly the one I should be talking to, you know."

"Why not, Dad? If you can't talk to your family, who can you talk to?"

"Ahh, Gloria." Barry sank back into his chair and leaned toward her. "I know how you felt about the farm. You thought I should have sold out years before I did. Even then I wouldn't have sold the farm, except that I wanted to give your mother something better than sixteen-hour days of back-breaking work. A woman deserves a certain measure of security, especially in the later years of life."

"You did the right thing, Dad."

"I thought so, in the beginning. But..."

"Yes?" This was the first time in her life that her father had opened up to her, and she sensed there was far more to this than met the eye.

"Oh, nothing. What's done is done. It doesn't look like the major will be back anytime soon. I'd better get home and help your mother with dinner."

"You? Help with dinner?" She could not hide her amazement.

"Well, it doesn't seem fair for me to retire and leave your mother with all the work. Anyway, I don't have anything better to do these days." His look was bleak. He'd changed in the five years since they'd moved to town. The brown eyes so like hers lacked sparkle. There was a slump to his strong broad shoulders. With a flash of insight, Gloria realized how much working the farm had meant to him.

Holding himself stiff with pride, Barry Russell came to his feet. "Tell the major I'll be glad to help with the painting. Just give me a call when."

"I will." She stood on tiptoe and pressed a kiss to his lean cheek. "Dad, you did the right thing."

His hand came up to awkwardly pat her shoulder. "I hope so. Now, I've kept you from your work long enough. Take some of your mother's cookies and get back to your computer."

Gloria did as he requested, but it wasn't easy to concentrate. She kept thinking about the look on her father's face when he'd insisted he was happy. When the phone on her desk rang, she picked it up with uncharacteristic eagerness.

"Doc! Thank God you're there!"

"Ross? Is that you?" She could hardly hear him.

"Yes." He sneezed, then continued. "I need your help."

"Where are you? And what's all that noise?"

"I'm at a truck stop off I-81."

"A truck stop? With the Stearman?" Amazement tinged the words.

"No," he replied impatiently. "The Stearman's several miles from here. I had to make an emergency landing."

"Oh, no! Are you okay? What happened? Is the plane all right?"

"One question at a time," he insisted. "I'm fine. It was the fuel line. And the Stearman's okay. I had just enough fuel left to land in a pasture near the interstate. I managed to hitch a ride with a truck driver to the nearest phone. Now I'm stuck." Across the lines, she heard him stifle another sneeze.

"I suppose you want someone to come get you."

"That's the general idea."

"I can call Stek for you."

"No, he has TDY."

"I don't like to sound like a greenhorn, but what on earth is TDY?" A tropical disease would be her first guess.

"Temporary duty. Out of town for the weekend, in Stek's case. Listen, Gloria. I need some tools. If I can fix the fuel line and get gassed up, I might be able to get the Stearman out of that pasture before sundown. How good are you at driving a stickshift?"

"Me?" He was going too fast for her. "Okay, I guess. But what does that have to—"

"Good," he interrupted. "I left the keys in my truck. Just back it up to my fuel trailer and—"

"Wait a minute!" she interrupted him. "I can't do that!" She didn't want to help him out. Gloria did not want Ross Adams depending on her. Depending connoted need and responsibility toward the other person. There was a distinct intimacy about the two emotions. Next, she might start needing him back—and that didn't fit into her plans for the immediate future.

"It's okay, Doc. There's nothing to hitching it—"

"I've pulled a trailer before!" Her jumbled thoughts made her snap back at him.

There was a moment's silence at the other end of the line. "Then what's the problem?"

She sighed. "Nothing." There was no way she could leave him stranded. "Look, why don't I use my car and pick you up? Then you can get your truck and go back tomorrow with someone who can help you fix the Stearman."

"No, you don't understand!" A sense of urgency filtered across the telephone wires. "I have to get the Stearman out of there as soon as possible."

"What's the hurry?" She'd never heard him sound frantic. It seemed out of character.

"The hurry is that the pasture looks as if it's used by cattle. If I miss my guess, they'll be heading that way as soon as the sun starts to drop."

"So?"

"So have you ever seen what a cow can do to a plane made from canvas and wood? The paint job is only a month old, for heaven's sake!" His distress was real. And so was another sneeze.

"Well, I can't imagine what damage a few harmless cows could do, but you've piqued my interest. I guess I'll just have to come out and see for myself. Besides, I can't have you coming down with pneumonia."

"I knew I could count on you, Doc! Now listen. The spare parts—they're in the . . ."

Gloria listened carefully to his instructions. Five minutes later, she was backing the truck up to the trailer of petroleum fuel. She wondered if all farm girls retained the ability to operate a tractor or couple a trailer to a hitch. She slid the trailer ball into its slot, then secured the safety chains. With deference to her volatile cargo, she pulled away carefully.

A half hour later, Gloria slowed and guided Ross's truck into the gravel lot of the truck stop. She had no trouble finding Ross. He was wearing his brown leather jacket and the red wool scarf.

"You made good time!" He jumped into the passenger's seat before Gloria could bring the vehicle to a complete stop.

"Don't you want to drive?" He brought with him the distinct scent of petroleum, its pungent odor filling the interior of the truck. The outline of flying goggles was imprinted around his eyes, making him look like a very attractive, if somewhat grimy, raccoon.

He sneezed and shook his head. "You're doing just fine. I'll navigate. Turn through there—" he pointed to a narrow alley between two lines of semis "—and take the west entrance back onto the interstate."

Squelching her nervousness, Gloria did as he directed. "It looks like you've been through World War

III," she commented as they flew along the interstate.

Ross pulled down the sun visor and peered into its mirror. Laughing at his image, he agreed and, using a handkerchief, wiped the fine sheen of oil from his face.

"There's our exit," he told Gloria. In less than five minutes, they were bouncing across a field to where the stranded biplane waited.

"The tools are in the back. Do you need help?" Slamming the door behind her, she joined Ross at the rear of the truck.

"Sure," he accepted. "You can bring these." She found her arms full of spare parts and rubber hoses. Toolbox in hand, Ross wasted no time in getting to the Stearman. In moments, he was unscrewing a metal panel directly behind the propellor. As he pulled the panel off, the pungent odor of gasoline enveloped them, but Gloria seemed to be the only one aware of the fumes.

"Just as I thought—a broken hose. See this?" He glanced over at Gloria who stood behind the left lower wing. "The fuel comes from the tank built into the upper wing. This thing—" he reached up and touched a glass cylinder that reminded Gloria of a hummingbird feeder "—is the fuel gauge. And these—" his hand moved to a series of tubes and hoses attached to a wing strut "—carry the fuel down to the fuel pump. If the line had broken up here, I'd have caught it sooner!" It was obvious he was angry with himself for getting into the predicament. Stifling another sneeze in his oil-smudged hanky, he gave a groan of disgust.

"And if I didn't have this blasted cold, I'd have smelled it!"

Unfortunately Gloria's cold was a thing of the past, and she wrinkled her nose as a cool afternoon breeze sent the petroleum odor her way once more. "Where did the fuel go to?"

"It was siphoned into the air." He directed a rueful glance down at his clothing. "I'm probably permeated with the stuff."

"I did notice a rather strong odor." Gloria tried to stifle a grin but it was no use. "I don't recommend it for everyday use as an after-shave."

Ross laughed out loud. "Well, this shouldn't take long to fix. Is there a crescent wrench handy?"

Gloria reached for the toolbox Ross had balanced on the running board. "Here." She handed him the appropriate item. As he worked on the problem, Gloria took a good look at the Stearman. It had two seats, one in each cockpit. Ross's name and rank were stenciled beneath the rear cockpit. Below and to the right of his name was a gold circle containing, of all things, a cartoon of a donkey. In front of the tail was the three-foot-high number, a 45. Another smaller 45 was painted on the nose. Her attention shifted back to Ross, and she noted the swift sure movements of his fingers as he attached a new length of hose in the fuel line.

"That does it!" he exclaimed as he tossed the crescent wrench back into the toolbox. He exchanged it for a screwdriver. "I'll put this panel back on. While I'm doing that, you could back the trailer up to the wing. Then we'll refuel this baby."

"Okay." Gloria resumed her place in the truck's front seat. The engine caught smoothly, and she shifted into reverse.

The crunch, when it came, was low and muted, but it had the effect of a rifle shot. Thinking at first that she had backed into Ross's precious plane, Gloria slammed on the brakes and bolted from the pickup. Ross's reaction was more direct.

"What the hell!"

As Gloria watched, Ross crouched and rolled beneath the wing, bounding to his feet on the opposite side of the fuselage. Satisfied that she had not rammed the Stearman with the truck, Gloria darted around the rear of the plane. A large brown-eyed jersey cow was blissfully scratching her eight-hundred-pound rump on the Stearman's fuselage. A cracked, dented fuselage, Gloria saw with dismay.

Another expletive from Ross told Gloria that he, too, had noted the damage. "Get out of here!" Ross's hand came down hard on the cow's rump. The animal gave out a sound of protest and lumbered away.

"Now I see why you wanted to get out of here!" was Gloria's immediate comment.

Scarcely winded by the unexpected exertion, Ross examined the damage. "Another foot and I'd have been minus a tail section," he muttered grumpily. "Where did she come from, anyway?"

"Over there!" Gloria pointed to the dozen or so cows making their way toward them. "How often does this happen?" she asked.

Ross's answer was a disgruntled shrug of his shoulders. "I don't know what it is about this plane—a natural back scratcher, I guess."

"Will she fly?" Together they checked the fuselage.

"Yes. If we get refueled and out of here before—" They looked up to see the herd of jerseys picking up their pace.

"Too late," Ross groaned.

"No, it isn't!" Gloria skirted the rudder section and made a beeline to the trailer hitch. In quick order, she had the safety chains unhooked. She lifted the chrome ball out of place, freeing the trailer.

She turned to Ross, who had followed her. "You refuel and get out of here. I'll take care of the wildlife. I'll meet you back home." She jumped into the pickup. Before Ross could agree or disagree, the truck went bumping across the pasture to head off the stampede.

At first Ross could only stare after the speeding pickup with Gloria at the helm. Then, delighted with her unexpected course of action, Ross did as she ordered.

Gloria angled the truck toward the herd of cattle. The animals bawled loudly as they realized she was coming between them and their goal. Slowing the vehicle, she leaned her head out the window. Using one hand to drive, she put two fingers of the other hand to her mouth. The subsequent piercing whistle brought the stampede up short. Pleased that the childhood ability had not deserted her in time of need, Gloria whistled again. Guiding the truck in a zigzag path, she kept it between the cattle and the vulnerable Stearman.

Finally she heard the sputter of the plane's engine. Another sputter, then it caught and held. She heard Ross call out her name.

She waved him on, and he wasted no time in taxiing away from the cattle. Gloria watched as he took to the air and circled back over the field. The Stearman swept low and as it zipped over her, the wings tipped from side to side in farewell. She returned Ross's jaunty wave, and as he flew north toward Blacksburg, she circled back to the trailer.

The cattle ignored her as she reattached the hitch, and standing alone in the field, listening to the cattle noises, she laughed out loud. It had been years since she'd had so much fun. Still smiling, she checked the safety chains, then jumped in the driver's seat and headed home.

Chapter Six

Gloria returned home at sunset. The hangar, with its soft, golden light spilling out into the quickly darkening night, was a bright beacon, and Gloria guided the pickup in that direction. Slowing, she drove in an arc and pulled up parallel to the wooden building. Before she could slam the car door behind her, Ross was at her side.

"You really surprised me out there, Doc, taking charge of those beasts the way you did!"

"As a former farm girl, I'll take that as a compliment." Pleasure from his admiring words rushed through her.

"Ahh, I thought I detected a pro."

"Actually, the one milk cow we had on the farm never showed a propensity for biplanes." She grinned at Ross, whose hair was damp from a shower. The petroleum scent of an hour ago was replaced by the distinctly masculine and pleasing aroma of a spicy cologne. "How is the Stearman? Any trouble in the air?" Side by side, they walked into the hangar, their steps taking them around the flying machine in a casual inspection.

"Everything is A-okay." Ross bent over and ran a hand over the dented fuselage. "These cracks are minor. I'll work on them later tonight."

"This plane is your obsession, isn't it?"

Ross straightened to find Gloria studying him. "A guy has to have something to fill his off-duty hours. Some men have wives and children, some are totally involved in sports. Others have a woman in every port—I have the Stearman."

"Funny, I would have put you in the next-to-last category."

"Professor," he chastised, raising both gold-tipped brows. "Shame on you for stereotyping. I realize that fighter pilots have a dubious reputation, and while I've done my share of hell-raising, I'm very picky about my women. And I'm very fond of this little lady." He patted the Stearman's fuselage with open affection.

"Then I'll leave you and your lady friend alone." She turned to go.

"Oh, no you don't." Ross firmly attached his hand to her elbow and guided her to one side of the wooden hangar. "It's not often that the damsel comes to the rescue of the prince. An appropriate reward is the order of the day."

"But I have work to do!" When he did not release her, she added, "And besides, I'm expecting a phone call—"

"The kitchen window is open," he pointed out. "We'll listen for it."

"But . . ."

"Look, Doc, everyone has to eat." He pulled out a chair and seated her at an old but clean table. With a quick flourish, he whisked a white cloth from the tray in the center of the table. "Dinner!"

A plate was placed in front of her. "The specialty of the house, a Reuben sandwich and hot tomato soup." Gloria's stomach growled in instant reaction.

"So," she mused as she eyed the stack of thinly sliced corned beef topped with crisp sauerkraut and melted Swiss cheese arranged on a baguette. It was a mouthwatering sight. "You fancy yourself as Prince Charming."

"What fighter pilot doesn't?" His grin was roguish as he took the chair opposite her. "Dig in while it's still hot."

Gloria did not have to be prompted again. The first bite was sublime and after swallowing, she sighed. "I don't remember the last time I was this hungry." She took a sip of the tomato soup. "This is great."

"And so were you to get me out of a jam."

Gloria dismissed his thanks with a wave of her hand. "Fair play—you rescued me from a vicious toy mouse—it stands to reason that I should save you from a herd of jerseys." A twinkle of humor danced in her eyes.

"Itchy jerseys," Ross amended with an affronted look.

"Itchy they were." A comfortable silence fell over the hangar as they companionably ate their meal. Ross finished his sandwich first. Shifting his chair at an angle from the table, he stretched his jeans-clad legs in front of him and crossed them at the ankles. The mug of soup fit in the curve of his hands.

"I take it you've forgiven me for dragging you away from your work?"

"Well," she said, feeling replete after the hearty meal, "just this once."

"You never told me you grew up on a farm."

"We never seem to find the time for casual conversation."

"That's true." He regarded her with curious eyes. "So what was it like? I'm a city boy," he added.

Gloria glanced thoughtfully into her mug before draining the last of the soup. "It was great while I was young," she admitted, setting the empty mug aside. "My brothers and sister and I had all the space in the world to explore." Meeting his eyes, she admitted honestly, "But that space became very limited as I grew older. And life became harder, especially if the year's crops didn't come in." She brushed aside his look of concern. "Oh, we kids never suffered. It was my mother who did that, almost as if it were her chief occupation. When I think of the long, back-breaking hours—the things she went without—" Her eyes clouded at the memory, and she looked down to study the worn wood of the table. "Let's just say it's not a way of life I'd recommend."

"So you left the farm for the hallowed halls of academia—a safe, secure way of life."

Gloria looked up sharply, remembering that he faced danger every day of the week. "There's nothing wrong with wanting to be safe or secure."

"No, I didn't mean to imply that there was," he said gently. His eyes met hers. "In fact, I'd highly recommend it."

She was wary of his words. "That's surprising, considering your line of work."

"I guess it is," he agreed. "I'll have to be honest—before I went to Southeast Asia, I'd never have said something like that—I couldn't understand why anyone wouldn't want a life of high adventure."

There was something deep in his eyes that compelled her to ask, "Something happened over there?"

"Men died—" his voice remained level, but there was a new intensity to his speech "—that's what happened. Men with wives and babies." He turned the mug round and round in his hands, staring into the liquid as he remembered. "My best buddy from flight school was one of them."

"How terrible for you."

Ross looked up and met her troubled gaze. "When I rotated back to the States, I went to see my buddy's wife. I'll never forget the look in her eyes—the pain, the hopelessness. She lost the person she loved most in the world and was left to raise two small children on her own." Gloria watched as a fire ignited in his deep blue eyes. "That's when I decided that a man in my line of work has no business with a wife and family!"

"I can see why you feel that way, Ross, but isn't that a bit unrealistic, asking a man to choose between a family and a career? He shouldn't have to make a choice."

"Maybe, but if I ever got in that position, I'd have to choose one or the other, but never both. It's asking too much of a woman to endure a life of uncertainty and sacrifice. Frankly, it's a rotten way to live. Military families are like Gypsies—there's no stability, no continuity, and then there's the anxiety." A deep furrow creased his forehead. "Always the anxiety, wondering day by day if their loved one will come home at the end of the workday. If that's not bad enough, there are always the weeks on end while the military member is pulling alert in some godforsaken hangar in the middle of nowhere or has been sent halfway across the world on TDY."

"You paint a rather grim picture of military life, Ross. If it's that bad, why do you stay?"

He shrugged. "Because the life-style suits me. I can do what I love doing best—flying one of the world's most sophisticated aircraft. And there's something to be said about living a nomadic life—for one thing, I'm never bored. And I've seen the world, experienced different cultures. I can enjoy that kind of life simply because there is no one sitting on the sidelines worrying about me. I have no one to answer to except my commanding officer."

"Do you ever worry about the danger?"

He nodded his head. "The element of danger makes me a better pilot—it keeps me on my toes, you might say."

The man fascinated Gloria. "I'm surprised you took this teaching job. It must be very tame in comparison."

"Not really. I've already found teaching challenging. You see, Gloria, I've combined my love of flying with my dedication to my country. For me, the old Strategic Air Command motto holds true: Peace Is My Profession. That may sound corny, but if I'm able to impart that belief to my students, then my three months here will be a success."

"Make peace, not war, hmm?" His professionalism drew her admiration.

"You'd better believe it—it's something I care very deeply about!" Face intent, he leaned toward her, then drew back. A glimmer of humor replaced the fire in his eyes. "Hey!" He stretched to put his empty mug on the table. "How did we get so serious?"

"We were talking about my life on the farm," was her reminder.

Ross chuckled. "Ahh, yes." His eyes focused on Gloria's face and he was silent for a long, thoughtful moment. "So now that you know why I'm still footloose and fancy-free, how about you? What's your excuse for not having a husband and a couple of cute kids?"

"Oh, I'm too busy right now—but I want a family of my own someday. When the time is right." It was Gloria's turn to ponder the life she'd chosen for herself. "I've planned my life very carefully, and step by careful step, I'm achieving my goals. Right now the important thing is to finish my project. It's been a real bear at times, but like you, I like a challenge. I should finish up by the beginning of the summer. After that, I'll take a well-deserved vacation before returning to the classroom in the fall. I plan to get tenure before I make any changes in my life."

"You like teaching?"

"I love it."

Ross nodded with satisfaction, then, his eyes never once leaving her face, he said, "Tell me something,

Doc, don't you ever get bored with all that paperwork?"

"No." Not until lately, she thought to herself, surprised at the idea. And she wasn't exactly bored. Distracted was more like it.

"If it were me, I'd be thinking of something more exciting to do."

"I thought the military was riddled with paperwork and red tape," she teased.

"It is," he agreed, raising one brow in his irascible way. "That's why I know what I'd be thinking of."

"And what's that?"

"Flying, what else?" He glanced toward the Stearman. "I'd be half a man if I had to give it up."

Gloria looked at the biplane, her expression less than enthusiastic. "Defying gravity is definitely not my idea of enjoyment, Ross."

"Then let me guess." He cocked his head as if to study her. "You're a prudent, methodical woman, but behind that professorial facade, I detect a propensity for mischief. I say that you'd be thinking of climbing one of those apple trees out back."

She tried not to grin at the idea. "I'm too old for that!"

"Really?" As if perplexed, he rubbed his chin. "Ahh, shopping! Isn't that what women like to do best?"

"Shopping! Come on, Major, can't you do better than that?"

"I'm trying my best, Doc." He snapped his fingers. "I know! Dancing! And don't tell me you're too old for that, because I'd refuse to listen!"

Before she could protest, he was standing up, grasping her hand firmly in one of his. "Come on, you've been spending too much time with that bucket of bytes you call a computer. I'll show you what you've been missing—"

"No, Ross." Gloria tried to pull her hand away. "You made it very clear the other day that you didn't want to dance with me." Disgruntled, she remembered the way Margie had enjoyed being in Ross's arms.

Ross's voice was low and serious as he regarded the frown on her face. "I wanted very much to dance with you then, and I want to dance with you now." Ross pulled her with him to a dimly lit corner of the hangar where the old Victrola was stored on top of a chest of drawers. Quickly, before she could escape, he turned the crank. Reedy, lilting music flowed out into the room. The next thing she knew, Gloria found herself in Ross Adams's arms.

The song was a fox-trot. The man moved with natural grace, and Gloria surprised herself by not tripping over his feet. Instead, she held on tight, one hand gripping his shoulder, the other grasped tightly in his. Their limbs moved in synchronization across the concrete floor.

Ross swung her about sharply, and the motion brought her even closer to his body. Giving her no time to catch her breath, Ross swept her across the floor. Together they moved in time to the lively tune.

"There!" Ross exclaimed softly when the music stopped. "Isn't that more exciting than working all hours of the day and night?" It was a gentle scold.

"You should talk—" she gasped. "You spend every off-duty hour working on your plane." It was very difficult for Gloria to think straight: the music had faded away but Ross was still holding her tightly in his arms. She was out of breath, her cheeks were flushed, her hair mussed. And she felt absolutely wonderful.

"Temper, temper," he scolded her, smiling down at the woman in his arms. She was warm and soft and fitted perfectly to the hard lines of his body. Holding her like this, inhaling her sweet scent—well, it was like pure heaven, he thought. It felt so right, so good. His restless spirit seemed to find peace in her presence. And yet the sensations she stirred in his body could not be termed as peaceful. Far from it. It was puzzling, these contrasting emotions. His feelings would have to be taken apart and analyzed—later, when he could think straight again. Right now all he wanted to do was be with her, hold her, kiss her...

She stirred in his arms and he remembered that she did not want to be kissed. Not by him, at least. She'd made that perfectly clear the other night. But keeping his distance, suppressing all his natural instincts was getting harder and harder to do. Looking down into her flushed face, he felt again that irresistible pull.

He lowered his head to bring his face closer to hers. With single-minded purpose, his gaze caressed her full pink lips. He remembered vividly how soft they'd felt beneath his, how sweet tasting. A sharp craving gnawed its way through his body. The shrill sound in the distance was slow to penetrate his thoughts.

"The phone, Ross." Gloria stirred in his arms.

"What?"

"The phone. I have to get it."

"Let it ring." His hands moved up her arms.

"It might be important," Gloria protested. The heat of his fingers seared through the thin fabric of her blouse. Another few seconds and she'd burst into flames. "It might be for you—another recall," she added breathlessly.

Ross's gaze shifted from her mouth to her eyes. "What a time for logic," he said with a sigh. "But you're right." His arms dropped to his sides, releasing her from his embrace. It was Gloria's signal to dash across the darkened yard and into the house. Gasping for breath, she picked up the kitchen phone.

"Dr. Russell here." She listened carefully for a long minute, then, with a quick thank-you, hung up the receiver. Turning, she saw that Ross had followed her and stood waiting at the kitchen door. "It's the call I've been waiting for, from Tokyo. They're getting ready to transfer some information to my computer. I just have to get it ready."

Ross followed her down the hall and into her office. He watched her go through the motion of setting up her equipment.

"Don't these computer people ever sleep?"

"It's daytime in Japan." The phone rang once before activating the modem. Lights on the terminal oscillated in response to the transmission coming in from the other side of the globe. "This is so much quicker and cheaper than sending this volume of information through the mail," she explained. The computer terminal clicked and hummed and then went silent. "Finished," said Gloria. "Later tonight I'll view and sort this stuff and tomorrow I'll start to weed out what I don't need."

"Aren't you going to take a day off from all this? Or at least get a good night's sleep?"

"Probably not—and I know what you're thinking—" She turned toward him and leaned back against the edge of her desk. "All work and no play, hmm?"

"Will never make Gloria a dull person," he finished with a smile. "It's just that everyone needs some time off. That way when you come back to your desk, you'll be refreshed and able to work with new perspective."

"You're a fine one to talk. You go from your air force job to your airplane out there."

"Flying the Stearman is the complete opposite of my military flying," he explained. "No schedules to worry about, no alert duty, no particular mission in mind except to enjoy myself. When I come back down to earth, I'm completely refreshed and ready to meet the next day with renewed vigor." As he spoke, he moved closer to Gloria, and in his eyes she could see sparks of excitement. Just talking about his passion seemed to light a fire inside Ross Adams. "I wish I could explain to you how I feel up there," he continued. "It's really something you have to experience for yourself in order to understand." He stopped short, then urged suddenly, intensely, "Go up with me tomorrow, Gloria and let me show you what I'm talking about."

"Go up?" He couldn't mean... Her mouth went dry as her incredulous eyes met his earnest ones. "No!"

"Yes." Ross was determined to change her mind, and it showed on his face. "Come with me in the

Stearman and I'll show you a wonderful new world! Oh, I'm sure you've flown commercially before, but this is different. Once you've seen the earth from an open cockpit, once you've felt the moisture of the clouds clinging to your face, you'll never be the same!"

Irritation skittered through Gloria. How could she make this man understand that she was perfectly happy the way she was? Right now, all she wanted was the peace and quiet to finish her project. "That machine of yours is dangerous!"

Ross did not deny her observation. "An element of danger makes it all the more exciting."

"To you. Not to me. Up there you're at the mercy of that machine, not to mention the raw elements."

"And you like to keep your feet planted firmly on the ground, to be completely in control of your life."

"Now you've got the idea." Blue eyes held brown as they assessed each other.

"Come on, Doc! All that security can get pretty boring. Some things are worth the risk! You'll come back stimulated, I guarantee it."

It wasn't necessary to go flying with Ross Adams to be stimulated, Gloria thought to herself. Less than sixty seconds in his company had her blood rushing through her body, bringing her alive and tingling with sensations she never knew existed. Perhaps the danger she sensed was not in the aircraft, but in the pilot.

He was waiting for a response. "That . . . that thing out there is made of wood and wire. Why, it's practically an antique! It should be retired to a museum."

Her declaration hit a nerve, and he pulled himself to his full height. "The biplane is hardly an antique!

In fact, there are four companies in the United States today that are still manufacturing models with two wings, and I'm not talking about restoring or renovating old ones. Biplanes aren't just used for sport, either. They do serious work."

"But look at how fragile it is—why, you weren't even safe from a half-grown cow!"

"On the ground, maybe," he admitted grudgingly, "but in the air you end up with a very maneuverable airplane that's light yet much stronger than a monoplane of the same weight. Crop dusters love it for its slow speed and low altitude control. Have you ever seen the Ag-Cat those guys use? They fly under telephone wires with it!"

Gloria shivered at the thought.

Ross noted her reaction and added, "There isn't a safer plane in existence."

"But there's always the off chance—like today—that something could fail."

"Yes." Several steps brought him closer to Gloria. "But what most people don't realize is that the biplane's crushable wings actually act as a crash helmet. It's the kind of plane you can wipe out and walk away from without a scratch. I'm safer in the sky than I am on the streets of Blacksburg. And with you in the cockpit with me, Gloria, I defy anything to go wrong." And it was true—with her safety and well-being in his hands, Ross felt he could keep the Stearman up with the sheer force of his willpower. He wouldn't let anything happen to this very special woman who fascinated him more every day.

Gloria stared at Ross. Just talking about flying filled him with energy. The animation lighting his handsome face was intriguing. It made her wonder, for the briefest moment, what it would feel like to reach out and touch a cloud, to hold a piece of the sky in her bare hand.

Reason quickly asserted itself. "No!" At the flash of disappointment on Ross's face, she added quickly, "Let's face it, Ross, I'm an earthbound soul. I want to control my own destiny. Besides, I have work to do, so I don't have time to fly away with you! Surely you can understand?"

"No, I don't, but I can see you've made up your mind about the subject. So—what do you say we get back to our party?"

"You didn't hear a thing I said, did you?"

"A couple of dances will hardly affect your work schedule." The shimmer in his blue eyes was a challenge.

Gloria refused to back down. "Dancing is not really my thing." In reality, she was torn in two, one part of her wanting, indeed needing, to be in his arms, the other part of her eager to get back to what counted most: her work.

"I don't believe that. With a little more practice, you could be a regular Ginger Rogers."

His statement made her laugh, and she instantly forgot her eagerness to see what her colleague from Japan had compiled. "To your Fred Astaire, I suppose."

"Now you're catching on." Ross reached to the bookcase where a portable radio vied for space with thick leather-bound books and plastic diskette cases. With a swift turn of his wrist, slow dreamy music filled Gloria's office.

"One last dance before this Prince Charming turns into a pumpkin," he implored.

"You're the furthest thing from Prince Charming that I can think of." He was a rogue, charming, good-looking, but nothing like the kind of man she planned to have in her life.

"I'm crushed."

"You are not—if Cinderella came along and started to talk about coming to live in your castle, you'd hop in that crate of yours and hightail it out of here as fast as you could!"

"Probably." He laughed and reached for her. As he took her into his arms, all thought ebbed from her mind. There was nothing else in the world but his fingers sliding around her waist. Her hands floated to his shoulders. At the same time, Gloria's lashes fluttered down as she savored the delicious sensations washing over her.

As one, they swayed to the evocative music. The room was small and cluttered with neat stacks of paper and sophisticated electronic equipment, giving them limited space in which to move. Not that it mattered: they were content to dance in a small circle, savoring the way their bodies brushed against each other. Her breasts were pressed to his chest, her hips swayed slowly from side to side, brushing against his torso with every step she took. His legs caressed the length of hers.

As the music faded, the announcer broke in with a commercial message. Slowly, as if awakening from a heavenly dream, Gloria opened her eyes only to discover her forehead nestled comfortably beneath Ross's chin. Her hands were firmly clasped behind his neck.

His fingers, splayed across her back, held her close. Slowly but surely, his hands started to move along her spine.

She must be crazy, Gloria told herself. She had just turned down Ross Adams's invitation to go flying because it was too dangerous. What was really dangerous was dancing in his arms. Why, here she was, holding on to him as if... as if they were lovers! The idea shocked her, but not enough to make her pull away. On the contrary, the idea was intensely intriguing. Being in his arms was wonderful. It had been so long since she'd been close to anything except her computer. She thought about how different she and Ross were. He was not a Prince Charming; he was the Red Baron. And she certainly was no Cinderella. Both of them were too old for fairy tales. They were adults with lives, careers of their own. They were human with human frailties and desires. She tilted her head and the movement brought her lips a breath away from his.

"Ross," she sighed, feeling distinctly light-headed and loving the sensation. "I think..."

"I know," he responded in a husky whisper. His hands tightened around her waist. "I know. You have work to do and you want me to go now." He released her and stepped back.

His words were like a shock of ice water dashing across her heated skin, restoring Gloria's good sense in an instant. That wasn't what she had been about to say at all! She had been about to tell Ross that she wanted him to kiss her. She felt anger at herself for wanting it, and she was angry at him for making her want him.

"Yes," she agreed with him quickly. "I want you to go." Watching him walk to the hallway, she reminded herself who she was: a career woman with no time for a personal relationship with a man who was all wrong for her. In a cool, impersonal tone she thanked him for dinner.

He stopped for a brief moment to glance back at her. "Thank you for the dance. And, Gloria, if you get tired of your electronic friend in there and want some flesh-and-blood company, just let me know. The offer to go up with me in the Stearman stands. Don't be afraid to change your mind."

"I won't change my mind!" She glared at him, thankful for the anger he so often stirred in her. It was like a protective barrier, this anger, shielding her from the force of his personality. The man had swept into her life, bringing with him his dancing blue eyes and an easy winning smile—not to mention his noisy, well-meaning friends and the phone calls in the middle of the night. All were interruptions that she could not afford. A relationship with Ross Adams would be courting the worst kind of danger.

Even as she thought of these things, the corners of his eyes crinkled in a rueful smile. "What a stubborn woman you are," he mused.

"I'm not stubborn, I'm determined."

His laugh rolled out and enveloped her. "That, too. And if I don't go now, I'll be tempted to come back in there and show you exactly who is determined around here."

"Tell that to the marines!" she called after him.

Chuckling to himself, Ross strode out of the farmhouse and into the spring night. He stopped to breathe the fragrant air. Stars sparkled above his head.

Ahead of him was the hangar, its light flooding the neat lines of the Stearman.

Behind him was a beautiful woman with the most incredibly stubborn tilt to her chin. His smile faded and suddenly he felt torn in two. The biplane represented everything he valued in life: excitement, high adventure, the taste of danger. The freedom to defy the odds, to pit himself against nature and win. He had no one to answer to but himself.

Then there was Gloria. She represented all that he'd put behind him long ago, and that included the warmth of a close and lasting relationship with a woman. The absence of a wife and family had left a decided gap in his life, but it had been something he'd been able to live with. Until lately. A man was meant to have a woman. One woman, a partner in life. It was as natural as the rain and the sun and the clouds he loved so much.

The acknowledgment of his innermost feelings was painful, and for the first time in his life, Ross Adams regretted being the free-spirited, danger-seeking man he was. Things could be so simple if he and Gloria could have a casual affair—a brief fling just to get her out of his system. It had worked with other women. But Gloria was nothing like the other women who had come and gone in his life. She was entirely different. And his feelings for her were different, too.

It was those feelings, running quiet and deep, that made Ross know that an affair was not the way to forget Gloria Russell. Filled with a restless energy, he strode into the hangar, coming to a sharp halt beside the Stearman. This was the only lady he wanted in his life. His hand moved across the fuselage. They had something in common, he and his flying machine. Not like him and Gloria. They were at opposite ends of the spectrum. He thrived in a world fraught with risks, and she was not a risk taker. Their goals in life were completely opposite. Gloria Russell, Ross told himself, was definitely off limits, and he'd do well to remember it.

He closed his eyes only to be assaulted with images of Gloria: angry when, in front of her date, he held up her freshly washed lingerie. Laughing when she realized she'd been frightened by a toy mouse. Beautiful and oh so desirable in her thin cotton nightgown—her concern turning to irritation when she discovered she'd rushed to awaken him for a telephone recall and not a national emergency.

And tonight, the look on her face had been soft and dreamy as she'd given herself up to the music—and his arms.

His pulse quickened at the recent memory.

"Hell," he said out loud, thrusting his hands into the pockets of his jeans. "Who do I think I'm kidding?"

Chapter Seven

Gloria threw open the window to the freshness of the morning air in hopes of dissipating the stuffiness in her office and clearing her sluggish mind. Seating herself again in front of the glowing computer screen, she took care to listen for the washing machine completing its cycle. The data from Japan was excellent. In fact, Gloria was amazed at the comprehensive scope of information her colleague had compiled. She'd worked far into the night in an effort to organize the material, and now, bleary-eyed and weary from too little sleep, she was having difficulty concentrating.

The washing machine clicked off. Rubbing her eyes, Gloria hit the escape key and exited the word processor. She then removed the data disk, sliding it into its protective sleeve. Knowing when to quit, she switched the computer off. Coffee and physical activity were the order of the day.

Setting her mug of hot coffee on the dryer top, she removed the load of clean sheets from the machine. As she paused to take a sip of the dark liquid, she became aware of the brilliance of the sun, the sapphire quality of the sky. A perfect day to dry her sheets on the clothesline.

Carrying the laundry out in a wicker basket, she pinned them to the line stretched between two trees behind the house. The illusive scent of apple blossoms lingered in the still air. In the orchard, birds called to one another as they flitted from tree to tree.

Gloria stood in the backyard, savoring the warmth of the sun on her face. The creaking sound of the hangar door sliding open intruded on her thoughts. In another moment, the coughing of a powerful engine split the peaceful atmosphere of the Sunday morning. The cough quickly turned into a loud roar. With a frown, Gloria watched the Stearman taxi out of the hangar. Ross, bareheaded and smiling, caught sight of her and waved before turning back to the controls in the rear cockpit. The plane turned abruptly to the right. The maneuver sent bits of grass and dust swirling into the air. Right onto Gloria's clean sheets.

"Ooo—you—I—" As she stood muttering a few mild expletives beneath her breath, Ross brought the plane to a halt. Leaving the engine idling, he jumped out of the cockpit to run back into the hangar.

As Gloria contemplated giving Ross a piece of her mind, Jane appeared to meander beneath the Stearman's wheels. The cat, completely unconcerned with the noise of the engine, jumped onto the lower wing and quickly disappeared into the forward cockpit. It was apparent to Gloria that Ross was ready to take to the skies without any idea that the cat was hitching a ride.

She quickly dashed to the open hangar door and called to Ross. He was nowhere to be seen and did not answer. Anxious for the animal's safety, Gloria turned to the aircraft. It looked incongruously like a dragonfly poised for flight. Gloria called to Jane.

No answer. She moved closer to the fuselage, calling again. Still no answering meow. Hesitating, Gloria hopped onto the metal footstep at the base of the lower wing and leaned into the cockpit.

"There you are!" The animal was crouched just out of reach beneath the seat. "Come on out, you crazy cat!" Gloria reached for Jane, who moved even farther out of reach. The only way to get the animal out of there was to climb into the cockpit and forcibly remove her. Gloria swung one leg into the cockpit then another and slid down into the leather seat. With the control stick between her legs, it proved more than difficult to get to the cat.

"I've got you now!" Gloria puffed.

"Here, let me help you." At the sound of Ross's deep voice close to her ear, Gloria jerked in surprise and lost grip on the squirming animal.

"That's all right." Gloria raised her head and darted Ross a quick glance. "I can get—" Before she knew what was happening, Ross reached around her and wrapped her in the seat restraint.

"What do you think you're doing?" She had to yell to be heard over the noise of the engine.

"I'm helping you with your seat belt."

"I don't need help, thank you! I mean, get that thing off me! I just got in to get Jane!"

Ross looked as if he hadn't heard her right. "Jane? I don't see her—ohh." He gave Gloria a knowing smile. "Don't be embarrassed about changing your mind, Doc. I understand completely. Here's your helmet. There's an intercom in the earflaps so we can talk—"

"Talk! How about listening for a change!" She jerked the leather cap from his helping hand. "I got into this crate for one reason only, and that is to get Jane out of here before you take off."

"Oh, don't worry about Jane. She's a seasoned traveler, although I do prefer her to be in her carrier."

"I thought so." Gloria fumbled with the buckle, which would not separate, no matter how she yanked on it. "I'm getting out of here!" The buckle flew apart. "Now will you please step aside?"

Ross did not move. "But Gloria, I finally have you where I want you."

"Let me out!" she repeated, raising her voice.

Ross tilted his head to one side in a very engaging manner. "Come on, now. Admit it—you've been wondering what I find so fascinating about this plane—what attracts me to the open skies."

Gloria opened her mouth to argue, then clamped her lips shut for a long frustrated moment. When she finally spoke, once more raising her voice to be heard over the engine, she sounded resigned. "All right, all right! I can see you're not going to let up! Yes, I'll admit that I've wondered what you find so irresistible up there!" She looked skyward.

Ross's face lit up. "Good! It's time you found out that there is more to life than a computer screen." He quickly resnapped the protective harness around her torso.

Her hand grabbed at his. "Ross, no! Just because I've been curious doesn't mean I want to go up!"

He took her hand in his and gave it a reassuring squeeze. "But you do want to go up, Gloria. I can see it in your eyes every time you look at my plane. You just don't want to admit the truth."

Gloria glared at Ross and tried to ignore how her heart was beating faster and faster, how her hand, tucked in his, was trembling at his touch.

"Do you?" prompted Ross.

"Maybe!" It was a grudging admission.

"You disappoint me, Doc."

"Okay! Yes! I mean, no—I don't like admitting it. I do wonder about this plane, and yes, I want to see what's so fascinating up there that it controls your entire life!" Her brown eyes blazed with fire as she blurted out the truth.

Ross met her gaze. "So you want to fly with me."

"Yes." It was a difficult admission. She brushed a lock of ebony hair from her eyes. "Don't just stand there gawking, Ross Adams. Let's get this over with."

"Yes, ma'am!" His right hand came up in a snappy salute. By the way he was pressing his lips together, it was obvious Ross was pleased with the turn of events. "Here, put this on." For the second time that day, he gave her the leather cap with its ridiculous earflaps. "We can converse through the intercom." He brought the straps under her chin and fastened it, the action bringing her face very close to his. He was freshly shaved and smelled of soap and spice, a delicious combination in Gloria's way of thinking. Gloria's eyes slid over the rugged lines of his tanned face. Not wanting to be caught staring at him, she craned her neck to look over her shoulder.

"Don't we need to switch places?" His gaze followed hers to the rear cockpit.

"Nope." He shook his head. "In this baby, the driver rides in the back." Quickly Ross gave her a rundown on the gauges displayed on the instrument panels, one facing her, the other mounted to her right. Then he took Jane and gently shooed her away from the Stearman. Before Gloria had a chance to change her mind about flying with him, Ross jumped into the pilot's seat and gunned the engine. Spewing more dust onto her clean sheets, the plane moved into position on the airstrip. The grass blurred as the craft picked up speed. As she steadied her shoulders, Gloria's gaze shifted to the front of the Stearman.

"Ross!" She'd practically screamed his name. "I can't see where we're going! Can you?" With the aircraft's nose-high attitude, Gloria's entire field of vision was filled with the massive engine and propellor.

"Relax!" Ross's deep voice was a soothing sound in her earphones. "I'm going to start steering side to side now, in an S pattern so I can see around the engine." The Stearman responded easily to his commands. Over her shoulder, Gloria watched Ross crane his neck first to the right, then to the left as he peered through the wing span to see where he was going. In his leather cap and familiar red scarf, he looked as if he knew exactly what he was doing. Noting her wide-eyed glance, Ross lifted one hand in a thumbs-up signal, indicating to her that they were ready for takeoff.

Facing forward, Gloria settled herself nervously in the copilot's seat. She felt Ross go to full throttle, and the entire world started to shake with a terrifying force. The noise from the straining engine was deafening. The ground whizzed by faster and faster as the wheels bounced roughly over the ground. Wind lashed Gloria's face. The air-speed indicator in her cockpit inched upward. Thirty-five, forty, fifty miles per hour and more. There was a sudden lift, and it felt as if she'd left her stomach six feet behind. The tips of the poplar trees at the end of the runway whizzed beneath them, perilously close to the fuselage.

Feeling sick, Gloria squeezed her eyes shut. "Ooo, how did I ever let you talk me into this—"

"You can open your eyes now, Doc. The view is great."

When Gloria finally peeked out at the world, her stomach had resettled itself. The violent vibrations had given way to a gentle rumble deep inside the machine. They were safely airborne.

The Stearman rose steadily into the blue Virginia sky. The view from Gloria's cockpit was incredible. Somewhere along the way, all the anxiety and tension had faded away, leaving a strange feeling of euphoria. Beneath the aircraft, rolling hills, vibrant with spring green, gave way to gently rounded mountains that seemed to go on forever. Thick forests resided harmoniously next to freshly plowed fields. Snaking highways crisscrossed the countryside, connecting one valley to another.

The plane leveled out, and Ross navigated to the south. In a matter of minutes, he was pointing out the Virginia Tech campus. Gloria recognized the buildings and eagerly identified them by name. Burruss, Lane, Wallace, Dietrick and Lane Stadium.

As they left the campus behind, Ross spoke to Gloria over the headset. "I'm going to take her up to eight thousand feet now." The engine surged with added power, and gradually the earth became smaller and smaller. "We're cruising at a speed of ninety-four miles per hour," he informed her. "Everything looks good back here: plenty of fuel, good oil pressure. How are things up there?"

Gloria quickly perused the gauges in her cockpit, wondering if he was asking for a status report on her instrumentation or if he was merely being solicitous toward his edgy passenger. "Everything seems just fine," Gloria finally replied.

The aircraft flew steadily south for about twenty minutes before Ross changed course to the west. He spoke suddenly. "Gloria, take the stick in your hand."

"Why?" Her quick question was a leery one.

"Just do as I ask."

Wondering if there was something wrong and he did not want to worry her, she did as he requested. "Okay, I've got it."

"Good. Now gently move the stick to your right."

Gloria complied. "Oh, my God!" she blurted out in panic. "We're tipping over. Ross, do something!"

His voice was completely calm. "Pull the stick back to the center." Gloria followed his direction. The movement halted the rolling motion of the aircraft but they remained gently tilted to the side.

"There now," Ross said. "We can see the ground better."

Gloria glanced to her right. "Yes—" she gulped "—that we can." The ground whizzed by at just slightly less than a hundred miles per hour. "Ross, I liked it better the other way."

He laughed. "Straight and level, huh? Okay, push the stick to your left and as we level out, bring it back gently to center." He paused as she carefully went through the motions he had just described. "Congratulations," Ross remarked as the plane righted its wings. "You just piloted the plane all by yourself."

"What?" Her hand jerked and the Stearman went into a dive. "Ross!" It was a cry for help.

He just chuckled softly. "You're the pilot," he reminded her as they continued to plummet toward the earth. "Pull up on the stick—easy, easy—"

Gloria overcompensated and the Stearman's nose went up—and up, into a steep climb. Suddenly there was a shudder and the plane felt as if it was going to drop to earth like a stone.

"We're stalling!" Gloria exclaimed in a near panic.

"No, we're not." Ross was completely unperturbed by the seesawing motion of the aircraft. "Come back on the stick just a tiny bit." Gloria was quick to respond, taking extra care not to overcompensate again. "A biplane," Ross went on in his calm voice, "is designed so that when the upper wings stall, the lower ones take over—like that." The Stearman lurched the tiniest bit and was back on a level course. Gloria breathed a sigh of relief.

"That was very good," complimented Ross. "Now you can relax that death grip on the stick. I'll take over for a while."

"How did you know..." She looked with surprise at the hand that was indeed tightly wrapped around the control stick.

"I'll never forget the first time I ever flew. My hand ached for days afterward." The words were warmly put.

Gloria laughed and relaxed, enjoying the feel of the plane's steady movements. Ross was right. Flying could be enjoyable once the initial shock wore off. And flying in an open cockpit was marvelously different from sitting inside a commercial airliner.

After a few minutes of steady flight, Ross asked, "Have you ever yearned to do a barrel roll?"

"I can't say that I have," Gloria responded dryly.

"It's less scary than a roller coaster," he pointed out hopefully.

"But a roller coaster is a heck of a lot closer to the ground."

"That's why it's safer up here at eight thousand feet. All that space between us and the solid earth."

"Don't remind me," she begged, then added, "but go ahead, do your barrel roll. I sense you won't be satisfied until you've completely scared the daylights out of me."

"You don't sound scared to me," Ross observed, "but I don't need to be asked twice. Okay, here's what I'm going to do—no surprises, I promise. Watch the movement of your stick as I roll us to the left." As he spoke, the plane easily moved onto her side.

Gloria sucked in her breath as the earth and sky tumbled, exchanging places. A second later, the Stearman completed the roll and the world righted itself once again.

"How did you like that, Gloria. Gloria?"

She gave a small laugh. "I hate to admit it, Ross, but that was fun!"

"Ever been on a roller coaster that makes an inside loop?"

"When I was a kid—"

"Are you game?" His voice was filled with suppressed excitement.

"I've come this far," she answered. "Let's go the whole nine yards."

Once again, the earth was above her head, the sky at her feet. A sense of exhilaration gripped her in place. "Again, Ross!" she cried and without even halting, he took the Stearman into another inside loop.

Next he executed a perfect roll to the left, then banked into a circle, taking them toward the east.

"It's your turn again," Ross offered after they'd leveled off once again. "Take the stick and fly her steady for a while." As she took control, he explained the relationship between the foot pedals and the rudders. Then he had her make a practice turn to the left, then a turn to the right.

"Now try a barrel roll of your own."

"I'm not sure I can do it, Ross."

"Don't worry, if anything goes wrong, I'll take over. We'll be completely safe."

"Okay, just remember, Major. You asked for it!" As Gloria rolled the biplane over, the nose pulled downward. A surge of panic went through Gloria as the craft went into a roll and at the same time spiraled toward the ground.

Ross's calm voice came to her over the headphones. "I've got it." Under her limp fingers, wrapped around the stick, she felt the plane respond and level out. "See how quickly the biplane responds," Ross pointed out. "It'll almost right itself."

Gloria gulped in great breaths of air and, letting go of the stick, clenched and unclenched her fists to keep her fingers from cramping. "What did I do wrong?"

"You didn't pull back on the stick to keep the nose up just before starting the roll. Keep your hand on the stick and feel its motion as I do a roll for you—" She barely had her hand wrapped around the stick when Ross sent the aircraft whipping upside down, then rightside up again.

"Okay, now you're going to do it again."

"I don't think so, Ross—"

"My hands are in my pockets—"

She knew he was not teasing and quickly took control of the aircraft. "Remember, up on the nose, then pull the stick forcefully to the left."

The Stearman rolled easily to the left and righted itself. "Ohh," Gloria breathed, pleased at her success. "Do you mind, Ross?"

"Be my guest." By the tone of his voice, she knew he was smiling.

Another roll smoothly accomplished, Gloria looked out at the horizon. "Oh, look, a cloud to the right! I'd like to..."

"Bank to the right, just the way I taught you."

Gloria maneuvered the Stearman into the center of the puffy white cloud. As they plunged out the other side, bits of moisture clinging to the wing tips, Gloria laughed with the excitement of the moment. Circling about the cloud, she pierced its moisture again, savoring the cool mist on her face.

"I could do this all day, Ross, but I see that our fuel level has dropped."

"So it has. Very observant, Doc. You have the makings of an excellent pilot." It was the greatest compliment he could bestow on a person, and she knew it.

Two hours after their momentous takeoff, Ross and Gloria taxied to a smooth halt on the farm's airstrip. As the sound of the engine died, Ross threw off his safety harness and levered himself upward to sit on the top of the fuselage. He pulled off the leather flying cap and ran a hand through his perspiration-dampened hair. "Whew, what a flight!" His grin was wide, his eyes filled with blue sparkles.

Freeing herself of the harness, Gloria stood in the cockpit and turned to Ross. "For once I agree with you." She grinned. "I had no idea it would be so...so..." She spread her hands wide and shrugged helplessly.

"I know what you mean—it defies description." Their eyes met and held in agreement, and once again Gloria felt the exhilaration she'd experienced high in the skies. She could easily lose herself in the blue depths of his eyes. He shifted his body toward hers and held out his hand. She took it and under his guidance, joined him on top of the fuselage. As she sat beside him, all her senses came alive. Adrenaline surged. Exhilaration ran high. Every nerve end in her body was tuned to the man who was lowering his head to hers. Her lips parted beneath his lingering gaze.

Ross had never felt this way. His every perception was heightened to an incredible degree. Sharing his passion for high flight with Gloria was having the most profound effect on his emotions. He'd never felt so close to a person. What they had shared just now, high above the earth, was more than special. It was something that came once in a lifetime. Her parted lips, pink and moist, sent a shaft of intense hunger and longing through his entire being. He bent his head, closer, closer. He was no longer willing to fight his craving for her.

"Hey, there, you two! We'd wondered where you'd gone to!" Margie's voice pierced the moment, shattering it as easily as the Stearman had shattered the vaporous clouds in the flawless blue sky.

Chapter Eight

I don't believe that's you up there, Gloria," Margie exclaimed incredulously. Behind her stood Barry Russell and the two Carter children, both of whom were staring with amazement at their young aunt crouched next to Ross on the fuselage of the Stearman.

Barry Russell was the only one who took the sight of Gloria in the leather flying cap in stride. "When you didn't show up for Sunday dinner, your mother got worried. She sent you something of everything. I put it in the fridge for later."

"Thanks, Dad. I would have been home for dinner, but this guy—" she jabbed a thumb in Ross's direction "—kidnapped me—forced me into this bucket of bolts against my will." She slid a few inches away from Ross.

"Really?" Margie looked at Ross curiously.

Unperturbed by the unexpected attention, the airman shrugged. "Your sister exaggerates. I did kidnap her, but only after I found her sitting in the cockpit, claiming she was trying to save my cat from a fate worse than death. Of course I knew she was itching to fly in my 'crate,' as she likes calling the Stearman." The corners of his mouth twitched in a suppressed smile.

Gloria's eyes twinkled back at him. "That's about the size of it," she agreed, laughing, and pulled off the helmet.

It was Ross's cue to leap to the ground, and he helped Gloria to find solid footing beside him. She introduced the major to her father and the two children, Karen and John. All three were obviously in awe of the Stearman, and Ross was quickly enlisted in giving the newcomers the aircraft's background as a military trainer.

"Would you like to go up and see how she handles, Mr. Russell?" Ross offered after the biplane had been thoroughly inspected.

"You don't have to ask twice, Major. And the name is Barry."

"Mine's Ross." The two men studied each other, each obviously liking what he saw. "We'll get going as soon as I refuel."

"I hate to miss this, but I have to go," Margie interrupted. "I have a date."

During the conversation, eleven-year-old John had been conspicuously quiet, but at his mother's declaration, he piped up. "Do you have to go? You'll miss seeing Granddad fly over the farm!" His face puckered into a frown.

"Oh, I can't, honey. Tony is waiting."

The frown changed to a childish pout. "He's all you care about anymore!"

"Johnny!" thirteen-year-old Karen scolded her brother. "Be quiet!"

Margie looked from one child to the other with surprise and concern. "John." She waited to get his full attention. "My going out with Tony seems to bother you."

"Yeah." The boy looked down and kicked a stone imbedded in the ground. "We were doing just fine by ourselves. We don't need some guy to come in and start telling us what to do. Then when he gets tired of having us around, he'll just drop us like a hot potato! We're better off without him!"

Gloria knew instantly that her sister had no inkling that her son felt so strongly about the possibility of another man entering their lives.

"Why didn't you tell me how you felt before this?" asked Margie.

"Karen told me I shouldn't make waves. That you'll lose interest in Tony soon enough." The boy's lower lip trembled.

"Karen?" Margie turned to her daughter. Karen's face reddened, but she was silent. "You two seem to have everything figured out. Did you ever wonder what would happen if I don't lose interest?" Margie's question was gently put.

"No!" John's chin stuck out stubbornly, and Karen's eyes widened with surprise at her mother's suggestion.

"Well," Margie told her children quietly, "you'd better give it some thought." With a hug to John's shoulders and a gentle touch to the top of Karen's head, Margie turned away.

"Margie," Ross called, his voice halting her halfway across the field. She turned. "Would you mind if I took the kids up for a ride, too?"

That caught John's and Karen's attention, making them forget their anxiety over their mother's relationship with Tony. Margie gave the invitation a few moments of thought. "I guess it would be all right. If their Aunt Gloria went up with you, you must be a pretty good pilot." She smiled at her children. "Yes—it's fine with me."

Both John and Karen let out a whoop of excitement. Margie waved and went on her way.

"How about a lift to the gas pump?" Ross asked the kids. In moments, he was helping the brother and sister into the forward cockpit. With Barry and Gloria looking on, Ross installed himself in the aft seat, got the engine going and trundled the Stearman carefully toward the fuel trailer.

It was an easy task to fill the wing tanks, then Ross guided the plane back to the runway. In short order and under the watchful eye of Barry and Gloria, the Stearman once again soared into the clear Virginia sky. The aircraft circled the farm, then carefully circumnavigated the valley before coming back to make a perfect landing.

"It's your turn, Granddad," John announced. He was the first to jump to the ground. "Aunt Gloria! We flew over the cascades! My friend Joey goes up there all the time to stay in a forest service cabin. It takes him three hours to hike up the mountain and it took us ten minutes!"

"I get the impression John enjoyed his trip," Gloria commented to Ross who remained in the cockpit.

"That's the last time I sit with him." Karen joined the Russell family on the ground. "He had me in a death grip the whole trip."

"I did not!"

"Look at my arm, Aunt Gloria! I'll be bruised for a week." The girl darted away from her brother, who lunged in her direction.

"Come on, kids," their aunt protested. "You'll make Granddad change his mind about going up."

"No, they won't," Barry denied, and with movements that belied his age, he scrambled into the passenger's seat. Ross handed him the spare flying cap and briefed him on the seat restraint and the gauges.

"See you guys later!" Ross and Barry waved from the cockpit and they were off, the sturdy biplane carrying them easily over the treetops at the end of the airstrip.

Before the Stearman touched ground again, the three observers were joined by a couple of handsome young airmen from Ross's office. Close behind came several gray-clad Virginia Tech cadets, talking eagerly of the day they would go off to flight training school. As Ross taxied the craft to a noisy halt, a crowd gathered to welcome the veteran flyer. Questions and pleas to go flying came at him from all sides.

Ross and Barry disembarked, the two men shaking hands congenially.

"What about it, Major?" A particularly bold young man edged himself forward.

"Sorry, fellas." Ross shook his head. "Barry here came to help me paint my kitchen. Some other time."

At the groan of disappointment, Barry intervened. "Ross, as I recall, that kitchen is no bigger than a mite. You go on and give these young fellas a ride. The kids and I will have your kitchen painted up in no time at all." The group cheered for Barry, some even patting him on the back.

"Are you sure, Barry? I hate to take advantage of you like this—"

"Nonsense! You took me for a spin in your biplane, and it was the most exciting thing that's happened to me in years. It's only fair I do something for you in return. Now go on, give these fellas the time of their lives, Ross. Come on, kids, we've got work to do."

"I'll come too, Dad," Gloria added. "I have some laundry to run through the wash again." She directed a speaking look Ross's way.

Catching her comment, Ross frowned. His glance settled on her mouth. A hunger gnawed at the pit of his stomach as he remembered the night not so long ago that he had returned several pieces of her laundry—and kissed her in the process. He wanted to do far more than kiss her. "I'll do those sheets over for you, if you have time to wait."

"No, thanks," Gloria replied hurriedly, disturbed by the glint of his eyes. "But if this keeps happening, I think we'd better set up a laundry schedule—to avoid mix-ups in the future."

"Whatever you say." Ross turned away, and as he tried to decide who would be his next passenger, Gloria fell into step with her father.

"You and the major having problems?"

"Let's just say that the major and I haven't quite worked out a good set of rules when it comes to sharing a washer and dryer."

"Aunt Gloria," Karen interrupted, "can I play some video games on your computer?"

"I thought you were going to help your Granddad to paint the upstairs kitchen."

"Not her," John said. "She's got two left feet."

"Since when does it take feet to paint?" Gloria quipped. The kids giggled. "I was planning on catching up on my work this afternoon, but I think I'd do better to get a fresh start on Monday morning—when the major and his noisy crowd of admirers are safely on campus." It was a rueful observation. "Go ahead, Karen. You know where the games disk is stored. I'll take your place behind the brush." And get to know her father better, she added silently, remembering their conversation the last time he'd come to the farm.

"Are you falling behind schedule?" Barry asked as they mounted the stairs to Ross's apartment.

"In case you haven't noticed, this place is beginning to resemble O'Hare Airport on a busy day." The roar of the Whirlwind engine drowned out her words. "With my front yard as the waiting room."

"I see what you mean." Barry laughed as soon as the noise faded in the distance, leaving only the chatter of young male voices to contend with.

The door to Ross's apartment was not locked. "Ross has done a lot with this place," Barry observed.

"This is neat!" John exclaimed, pointing to a small model of an F-16. Above an antique table hung a framed print of Willard Cox's *End of the 1st Round of the World Flight*. Depicting a biplane parked in a grassy field and surrounded by its leather capped pilots, it was just the kind of artwork Gloria expected Ross to have. The three stepped farther into the apartment. It had changed since the last time Gloria had seen it, the night of the recall. Not that she'd been in any state to notice the furnishings. She'd only been interested in getting away from the revealing light of the brass floor lamp—and Ross's gaze. Those sky-blue eyes had haunted her dreams at night and interfered with her work during the day.

"Don't touch anything, John," Barry warned his grandson. As the two set down the paint cans they had gathered on their way up the stairs, Gloria studied the rest of the apartment.

It was sparsely furnished and possessed a comfortable, masculine air. On a living-room side table was a small collection of regimental beer steins from Germany. A Turkish scimitar graced the adjacent wall. On the floor, which had been cleaned and polished to a high gloss, was a handcrafted Turkish carpet, its muted blues and grays giving the room a restful air. Arranged in a circle around the carpet was a grouping of chairs, all of which Gloria recognized as having come from Margie's loft.

Through the open bedroom door, Gloria noted a neatly made bed. The low bookcase beside the mattress was cluttered with an expensive stereo set, stacks of tapes, textbooks and papers. It was obvious that Ross graded papers in bed, she mused, recognizing the telltale signs.

"Gloria," her father called to her, "you can help by taking everything out of that bookcase. Might as well paint it along with the kitchen." The case he mentioned was a built-in divider between the dining and living area.

Working next to Barry gave father and daughter the opportunity to talk—really talk. Barry missed his farm, his work, he confided to Gloria. An idle life was not for him, but his love and concern for his wife had forced him to turn his back on the life he really loved. In the past, Gloria had been certain that her father had made the right choice by leaving the farm. But now, looking into his eyes, hearing the wistfulness in his voice as he entertained his grandchildren with anecdotes of life on the farm, she wasn't so sure. He was, she saw clearly, only half the man he used to be.

"A toast!" Barry raised his mug of coffee. "To a family project well done." A satisfied expression appeared on his face, making him seem younger and more energetic. By then, Karen had joined them, and she and John were drinking hot cocoa.

"That coffee sure smells good." Ross appeared in the doorway of his apartment.

"Come on in, Ross," Barry said, smiling. "This is your place, after all."

While Karen poured Ross a cup of coffee, Gloria checked the bookcase to see if it was dry. Discovering it was, she set aside her mug and quickly started to put back the assortment of books and framed photographs that belonged on its shelves. While Ross lingered in the kitchen, Gloria tried to remember where everything went—the wedding photo with Ross as a proud best man belonged on the top shelf next to a snapshot of himself as a young lieutenant in Vietnam. A more recent photograph showed Ross and a trio of smiling officers standing in front of an F-16. The next shelf was for a collection of leather-bound historical works with well-worn edges. Below that came an assortment of flight manuals and an up-to-date copy of *All the World's Aircraft*.

"Nice Job."

At the sound of his voice directly behind her, Gloria dropped the flight manual she was trying to replace. "I'm sorry!" She bent quickly to retrieve the book that had fallen open on the floor. At the same time she breathed in a deep gulp of air, which, instead of clearing her mind, filled her with Ross's special scent—fresh air, tangy after-shave and a hint of oil, leather and fuel. She shifted her attention rapidly to the book. A diagram of wind flowing up and over the wing of a biplane filled the pages.

"See this?" Ross bent beside her. "This is what I was telling you about this afternoon when you stalled out. See how the double wing works to your advantage?" He went on to explain more. Fascinated with the theory and the way Ross explained it, Gloria asked a few more questions. Ross leafed through the pages, easily explaining the aerodynamics of the biplane.

"We're all finished," Barry interrupted them. Gloria looked up to see her father rolling his sleeves down and buttoning the cuffs of his shirt. "I'll be taking the kids home now."

"I'd better go, too." Gloria stood up quickly.

Ross came to his feet with her. "Would you like to take this with you, Doc, and look it over for a few days?" He held out the flight manual. "It might help for the next time you go up." It was a definite invitation to go flying.

"Oh, I don't know if I'll have time—I have so much work to do, and I've fallen behind schedule."

"Sorry to hear that." There was a genuine flash of disappointment in his eyes. "But go ahead and take this. I won't be needing it, and you just might find some time for it."

"Well, okay. Thanks." She smiled.

"No—" his pleased look encompassed the entire Russell family "—I thank you. All of you. The place looks great." The five of them bade Ross good-night and Gloria left with her family, taking Ross's book with her.

The following week was a repeat of the previous one. She and Ross ran into each other on occasion, but they were never alone. He was usually accompanied by visiting friends or cadets anxious to see the Stearman. In a way Gloria was thankful, because she did not want to be alone with Ross Adams. There was no doubt in her mind that the man was a danger to her senses. In fact, she was relieved that the man drew a crowd wherever he went. There was safety in numbers, Gloria told herself. And yet, she couldn't help but wonder what would have happened up there on the fuselage if her family had not appeared on the scene so suddenly.

It was a thought she kept at bay as she busied herself with her work. April brought true spring weather. The green countryside was dressed with the pink and white native dogwood blossoms. Rhododendron and azalea rushed to flower even as the apple blossoms in the orchard gave way to tiny fruit on the trees. The world was changing at a rapid pace. Between computer printouts, Gloria watched the changes from a safe distance behind her office window.

One warm Friday evening in mid-April, there was a tapping on her office window. Turning, she saw Ross beckoning from the other side of the glass. She pushed back her chair and stretched aching shoulder muscles before raising the window.

"You look like you could use a breath of fresh air. Come on out and sit with us for a while."

"But..."

"No buts. You've done enough for today, and you can't hide in there forever."

"I'm not hiding! I'm working."

"Well, you work too hard. It's Friday night, and this office closes after eight o'clock, major's order." He was irresistible when he smiled at her in that cocky fashion of his. "Now hurry or you'll miss the sunset."

By the time Gloria powered down her equipment, the sun was indeed a deep red orb on the western horizon. Ross settled her into a lawn chair. One of his friends thrust a cold beer into her hand.

There was enthusiastic talk of an upcoming fly-in. A student brought up the subject of summer camp. A young sergeant amused them with an anecdote from boot camp. Slowly Gloria relaxed, thankful to let go of her work for a while.

As darkness closed in, the friendly crowd dissipated one by one until Gloria and Ross were the only ones left. They were silent for long minutes, each savoring the silence.

"I hope my friends haven't been too much of a bother—they can get a bit noisy," Ross finally said.

"Yes, they can, but thank goodness they're either in school or at work during the day," Gloria agreed. "I make sure I do most of my work when you're on campus. You're like the Pied Piper, you know."

She could not see his reaction in the darkness, so she continued. "Before you came to live at the farm, I worked straight through every weekend with just one break Saturday night and dinner with the folks on Sunday. But these days, I don't even try to work."

"Are you falling behind schedule?" His voice in the dark sounded concerned.

"A bit—but nothing I can't handle."

"If you're not working on weekends, what are you doing?"

"Besides avoiding the rush-hour traffic in my driveway?"

"Yes." She didn't have to see him to know that he was grinning.

"Oh, housework, laundry. I visit the folks, and I've been reading that book on aviation you lent me. Last night I stayed with Margie's kids while she went out with Tony."

"How's John handling it?" He remembered the boys vociferous objection over his mother's seeing Tony.

"Not much better, I'm afraid. His father's leaving them had a big effect on him. He doesn't trust easily." They fell silent.

A few minutes later, Ross asked, "What do you think of the book?"

"It was very easy to understand, and yet it wasn't in the least remedial. I've learned a lot." She didn't tell him that it was the most fascinating subject she'd encountered in a long while.

"It's the one I always recommend to people seriously interested in learning to fly."

"You think I'm interested in flying?"

"Aren't you?" There was a long pause as Gloria thought about it.

"Yes. I guess I am. Just one trip up and I really do understand how it can get in your blood."

"How would you like to go up tomorrow?"

"And compete with the Ross Adams Fan Club? I don't think so." Even through the darkness, she could feel his eyes on her face.

"You know," he mused, "before I went to Vietnam, I took a jungle survival course in the Philippines—one thing I learned was how to resist and evade capture."

"What are you getting at?"

"If we get up at sunrise, we could make a quick escape in the Stearman. We wouldn't have to come back until sundown."

"That sounds like a long day."

"We don't have to spend it all in the air. I'd give you some lessons, of course, then we could find a nice field—"

"Without jerseys—"

"Without jerseys. Spread out a tablecloth and have a picnic. Later we could find a creek and go swimming."

"That sounds tempting, but—"

"Are you watching the kids tomorrow?"

"No—"

"You have a date with Erik?"

"No—"

"Then what's the problem?"

The problem was that she wanted very much to spend a day with Ross Adams. He was like the sun, bright and enticing after a long winter of hibernation. The entire world was in the throes of spring, and she was the outsider watching from her office. Like a child with her nose pressed against the window of the candy shop, she craved what was on the other side. And now the door to the candy shop was being opened, and despite the fact that she knew she shouldn't indulge, she seized the opportunity.

"No problem," she denied. "I was planning on stopping over at the campus library, maybe visit with Mother and Dad. But I could do that another day. If you're asking me to go on a picnic, I'd love it."

Ross was surprised yet obviously pleased at her easy capitulation. "Doc, you've got a deal. I'll bring the fried chicken, you bring the potato salad."

"What makes you think I can make potato salad?"

"Instinct."

"Last time you relied on instinct, you assumed I would rather climb a tree than work."

"Oh, that. Barry and I had a little talk. He told me that when you were a kid you were the tree-climbing champ of the county." There was a certain smugness to his words.

"He told you that?" Gloria laughed. "I'd better have a word with that gentleman, letting out all my secrets."

"But you'll bring the potato salad?"

"Yes, I'll bring the potato salad, and you can bring everything else."

"It's a deal." It was their cue to stand up and walk back to the farmhouse.

"How does six o'clock sound?" Ross asked at Gloria's door.

"Too early," she declared, "but I'll be ready."

"You're being very agreeable tonight."

"Temporary insanity. It happens to all college professors about this time of year."

"I hope it's not too temporary." Before she could form an appropriate comeback, Ross loped up the stairs and with a "Sleep well!" disappeared into his apartment. Laughing softly, Gloria headed for bed.

Chapter Nine

"Temporary insanity was right," Gloria told Ross when she answered his prompt knock on her door the next morning. "I should have my head examined. I had to get up at four to get this potato salad ready on time."

"It smells great. Is that coffee I see over there?"

"Help yourself," Gloria replied. "There are doughnuts on the table. I'll be ready just as soon as I finish pouring iced tea into the thermos."

A scratching noise came from the kitchen door. Ross opened it, and Jane slipped through the space.

"Is she going with us?"

"Not a chance. I've been dreaming about being alone with one Gloria Russell since the day we met, and I'm not going to share you with anyone, not even Jane." There was something in the tone of his voice that made Gloria's eyes widen. Her mouth opened as if to protest, but he cut her off. "Don't worry, Doc. I'm an officer and a gentleman, remember? You'll be perfectly safe. So come on." He rinsed his coffee mug and gathered up the small cooler of food Gloria had packed. "Let's go before an early bird comes along and interferes with our plans."

"But you didn't have a doughnut," Gloria protested as he rushed her out of the house and toward the plane poised at the edge of the airstrip.

"We'll stop somewhere for breakfast."

In minutes they were soaring into the sky, leaving everything and everyone behind. The Stearman rose eagerly to meet the dawn. In the forward cockpit, Gloria had an unparalleled view of the sun stretching its golden rays across the edge of the world.

As Ross piloted the aircraft to the south, the sky brightened. Thick forests cast morning shadows across patches of adjacent fields where white-tailed deer grazed peacefully. A seldom seen black bear loped across an abandoned pasture.

"Where to?" Ross's voice was peppered with static in Gloria's earphones.

"Mabry Mill." Her response was quick and sure.

"Roger." Ross followed the snaking line of Highway 8. Below them, Gloria recognized the Little River and ahead of them the crest of the Blue Ridge Mountains. They picked up the parkway at Rakes Millpond and banked westward, following the winding road along the mountain crests that linked the Shenandoah National Park in northern Virginia and the Great Smoky Mountains National Park in North Carolina and Tennessee.

Gloria recognized landmarks along the Blue Ridge Parkway and pointed them out to Ross by name: The Saddle, Rocky Knob, Rock Castle Gorge, Mabry Mill.

Ross circled the water-powered mill and spotted a small airstrip. In moments they landed and parked. It was a short hike to the restaurant where they ate a hearty country breakfast complete with grits. Afterward, they took a leisurely stroll around the mill lake where the old water wheel was still in operation. They bought a small bag of freshly ground cornmeal and visited the blacksmith shop. Then it was back to the Stearman.

High above the southern highlands, Ross put Gloria through her paces, checking to see how much she remembered about her first flying lesson.

"You're the best pupil I've ever had, Doc!" Ross exclaimed after a successful barrel roll.

"I read that book of yours from cover to cover," she admitted, releasing the stick to his control. "Knowing the theory behind flying makes all the difference."

"You sound as if you're enjoying this."

"Oh, I am! It's so different from my life on the ground—not that I don't like my life, mind you," she amended quickly.

"Of course not," Ross agreed with her. "But you do have a tendency to stay in your little rut."

"You're calling my intensive research a rut?"

"Yup, and no need to get in a huff, Doc. Your research may be intensive and very important to you, but you can't enjoy doing it twenty-four hours a day, week after week." When she did not answer him over the radio, he added, "Come on now, admit it."

"I suppose I'll have to." And she surprised herself by laughing. "After all, you're in control of this bucket of bolts."

"Not now I'm not—"

She grabbed the stick and put her feet to the rudder controls just in time to curtail a dive. "Ross Adams, you're crazy!"

"Can't disagree with that, Doc." His chuckle was a warm deep sound in her ears. "Take her down to twelve hundred feet," he added.

At the requested altitude, Ross told Gloria to look out for a particular landmark.

"There it is," she pointed out ten minutes later.

"Good. Fifteen degrees west is a landing strip. It's nice and long. A perfect place to practice touch and go's. Take her down."

"Take her down? Are you talking to me?"

"Is there someone else up there with you?"

"Of course not!" Gloria failed to see any humor in his question. "I don't want to take this crate down!"

"Knowing how to fly won't do you much good if you don't know how to take off and land."

There was a long silence. "I'm afraid, Ross."

"Don't be, Doc. I'll be with you the whole way. In fact, give me the controls and I'll put this baby through her paces several times, then I'll let you give it a try. Are you game?"

Gloria moved her head to stare down at the ground. "Okay," she sighed, then loosened her grip on the stick. "I'm game."

Ross was all business as he banked and curved toward the airstrip. Lined up for a landing, the Stearman dropped altitude, its three wheels barely skimming the grass before soaring back into the sky. It was a perfect touch-and-go maneuver. As they repeated the action several more times, Ross explained the technique to Gloria, who remembered reading about it in the flight manual.

Then it was her turn to approach the field. The Stearman dropped altitude too fast and Ross calmly ordered Gloria to pull up on the stick. She did, and her first pass over the field was a high one.

"Again," Ross directed her, "but this time..." and he went into a calm, uncritical explanation of what she'd done wrong.

After three more passes, Gloria did a proper touch and go. Then Ross insisted she do it twice again.

"That's good," he finally told her. "Now this time, instead of pulling up, you slow her down and land. I don't know about you, but I'm ready for lunch."

"Lunch!" Gloria squelched a surge of panic. "How can you think of food at a time like this!"

"Easy. I know you can land this baby as well as I can. Take her down and remember everything we've talked about."

"You're crazy. No," she amended quickly, "I'm crazy to even contemplate this. No." She changed her mind once again. "We're both crazy."

Ross chuckled. "No arguments from back here. Now, check your air speed and altitude...."

Gloria focused her entire attention on the plane, hoping it would respond quickly when the time came.

Then there was no more time to even think—she only did, following Ross's reassuring instructions in detail.

There was a bump as they touched the ground, then the Stearman surged back into the air. Sheer terror edged its way up Gloria's spine, but Ross's calm voice halted its spread. She focused on the reassuring sound and brought the biplane under control. In the next minute, they were rolling to a jerky halt.

Ross was first to jump to the ground. He stared up at Gloria, who sat limply in the forward cockpit.

"Well, are you going to sit there all day, or are we going to have some of that potato salad?"

"There you go again," she said weakly, turning her head toward him, "thinking of food—" her voice became markedly stronger as she spoke "—when I've just landed this little beauty for the first time!" A surge of adrenaline brought color back to her face.

"A few minutes ago she was a bucket of bolts," Ross pointed out, a smile crinkling the corners of his eyes.

"She's a beautiful bucket of bolts, Ross!" Gloria patted the fuselage. "And landing her was the most exciting thing I've ever done in my life!" Releasing her safety harness, Gloria pushed herself up and out of the seat. Ross moved to offer a hand. It took a mere second to pull off her helmet and shake out her hair. A sense of supreme exhilaration swept over her as she put her hand in his. Dropping to the ground beside him, she lifted her face to his.

Without thinking, she laughed in jubilation and, reaching on tiptoe, kissed Ross Adams full on the mouth.

When he spoke, his voice was curiously breathless. "Was that for a successful first landing or was that for me?"

"That was for my landing." Brown eyes sparkled up at him. "This is for you." Her hands slid around his neck and pulled his head down. Her mouth once again sought the warmth of his, but this time, she leaned into his body and kissed him with a depth that sent a shudder through him.

Gloria forgot all about the milestone of a first landing. There was only Ross and the feel of his mouth over hers bringing her senses completely alive. All her perceptions were heightened and tuned to the man whose arms gathered her close. Her heart took wing and soared to heights never imagined in the Stearman.

"My God," Ross groaned when they finally broke for a breath. "I think I've died and gone to heaven."

"No way, Major." Her voice was husky with emotion. "That was no crash landing."

"Speak for yourself, Doc." This time it was his mouth being the aggressor, and Gloria met his passion with passion. She wrapped her arms tightly around his shoulders and pressed her body to his with elation. This was where she wanted to be, in his arms, surrounded by his gentle strength, tasting his desire.

His lips released hers only to rain kisses along her cheekbone and across her eyelids.

"Still hungry?" Gloria gasped at the shocks of electricity rippling through her.

"Ravenous," Ross growled and covered her lips, his tongue seeking entry to her mouth. A stream of molten heat surged through her bloodstream with volcanic swiftness. Her skin tingled as his hands worked another kind of magic—tracing the feminine contours of her form, his fingers stopping here and there to explore areas of particular interest.

Gloria felt as if she would burst into flames at any moment.

It took the low of a cow to bring them back to reality. They broke apart quickly, their eyes searching for the animal that had made the noise.

It was a guernsey, safely kept off the landing strip by a strong wire fence. Further examination of the area showed that the metal hangar was deserted. Ross and Gloria laughed with relief, their eyes meeting across the short space that separated them.

"Looks like we've got the place to ourselves," Ross said, keeping one arm around her waist. "Over there." He pointed to a small copse of trees. "It looks like the perfect place for a picnic."

"Yes, perfect," Gloria agreed.

Stealing one more brief hard kiss, Ross led Gloria to the storage compartment behind the cockpit section. Together they unloaded the cooler and picnic basket. Gloria carried the tablecloth to a shady spot beside a flowering mountain laurel. They spread the food across the cloth. Everything properly arranged, they sat side by side, very close but not quite touching.

"Iced tea?" Ross asked, reaching for a paper cup.

"What, no wine?" Her voice was still husky from the effects of their kisses.

Ross's eyes twinkled. "If I brought wine, you'd think I had an ulterior motive in spiriting you away from the farm."

"Oh, I see," Gloria mused. "I might think you want to get me tipsy and then you could steal a few kisses from the proper professor, hmm?" She smiled, her gaze running lovingly over his face. "Well, I fooled you, Major. My kisses are free of charge. And I know exactly what I'm doing." Her eyes held his, telling him she no longer wanted to fight the attraction between them.

He was quiet for a moment. "I heard from my flight commander in Florida last week," he said almost casually. "After the first of the year, my unit is being transferred to duty in the Pacific."

Her heart gave a little lurch. "How do you feel about that?"

A light gleamed in the blueness of his eyes. "It's what I've trained for. Its my job."

"And you're rejoining your unit in June." They weren't easy words to say, but she needed to hear them out loud.

His answer was a quiet but firm "Yes."

She took a deep breath and, still holding his gaze, said, "I'm looking forward to getting back to my job in the classroom come September."

"Maybe I'd better take you back to the farm—"

"No!" She put a hand to his cheek, loving the weathered feel of his skin on her palm.

His hand covered hers. "Gloria, I'm a transient. I have no business interfering in your life. And if I don't take you home right now, I'm going to kiss you again." The words were intense, full of meaning.

"I was counting on the latter, Major Adams."

"Oh, you were, were you?" He took her hand from her cheek and turned it palm upward. He pressed a quick kiss to the tender skin.

"Yes." She pulled her hand away and reached for the bowl of salad. "So here, eat some of this potato salad that I slaved over and stop worrying so much about the future."

"There is no future for us."

This time she did not meet his eyes. "I'll keep that in mind." She heaped a paper plate with too much salad.

"Just so you know." His fingers brushed her arm.

"I do! Now shut up and eat." She reached for a piece of fried chicken, holding it up in front of him.

"Yes, ma'am!" Ross bent forward quickly and took a bite of the meat, his teeth barely missing her fingers.

He picked up a piece of the crispy meat. "Your turn." He held it to her mouth. After she took a bite, he forked a helping of salad and offered it to Gloria. As she took it into her mouth, a chunk of potato fell into her lap.

Ross took a second bite of the chicken between her fingers. Gloria reached for a spoonful of pork and beans, losing half the tomato mixture on the way to his mouth.

"This looks easier in the movies," she said, laughing, after trying fruitlessly to take another bite of the chicken he held.

"You don't like my technique, is that it?" Ross complained good-naturedly.

She put down the piece of chicken she'd been trying to feed him and reached for a paper napkin. "I didn't think it would be so messy."

"Or so slow," Ross agreed with her. "At this rate, I'll starve to death!" He pulled his plate onto his lap and launched into the hefty serving of potato salad. After one taste, Ross sighed with satisfaction. "Your dad was right. This is the best salad I've ever had."

"Well," Gloria replied, claiming her own plate of food, "I haven't always hibernated behind a computer screen, you know."

"So I've been told." Ross turned and searched the grove of trees behind them. "See that tree over there? The oak with sturdy branches? I plan to race you to the top—after my food settles, of course."

"You're on. And don't sound so smug. My father wasn't kidding about my being a tree-climbing expert."

"I'll only believe it when I see it."

"Save some room then, because I'm going to make you eat your words."

Ross laughed and, in open defiance, downed a large forkful of salad and reached for a second piece of fried chicken.

Chapter Ten

"Hey!" Gloria called down to Ross from her vantage point at the top of the tall oak. "What do you have to say for yourself now?"

His face was partially hidden in the thick green foliage. "I say you're an amazing girl." One hand, then another, grasped the tree trunk, and Ross lifted himself onto the limb beside Gloria. They had a clear view of the pasture where the guernsey grazed on the verdant grass.

"I'm hardly a girl at age twenty-six."

"I know." The stout branch creaked as he shifted toward her. "You're a beautiful, irresistible woman." His hands came up to frame her face. "Do you have any idea how many hours I've lain awake in my bed upstairs, wondering if you were awake, too, thinking of me?"

"I've thought of you," she whispered. "I've thought of the night you first kissed me."

"Have you forgiven me for that yet?" He moved his head so that his nose touched hers in a gentle caress.

"No, but not for the reasons you think."

His attention shifted from the straight line of her nose to the curve of her ear. His tongue tasted the delicate lobe. Gloria closed her eyes as a million butterflies swept through her stomach.

"Why, then?" he asked into her ear.

She drew her breath in sharply. "Because you made me want another kiss, Ross." As she spoke, his mouth made a foray across her cheek to find the corner of her mouth, giving her a whisper of a kiss. "And another," she breathed, and before she could close her mouth, his lips settled over hers in a searing kiss. His arms went to her waist, drawing her close to his body.

Gloria's world shifted on its axis as his mouth took total possession. Her head whirled, her heart raced. A loud crack split the air.

"Ross!" Her arms around his neck tightened. "We're slipping!"

"I've heard of being swept off my feet," Ross exclaimed desperately, "but this is—" There was no time to finish his thought. As the limb gave way beneath their combined weights, Ross lunged to the branch below them. He caught Gloria in his arms just as their perch snapped in half and went crashing to the ground.

Gloria clung to Ross's neck. "I think something is telling us that we're too old to be making love in a treetop!"

Helping each other and laughing at their close call, they carefully made their way to the ground and, hand in hand, ran back to their picnic spot.

Breathless and laughing, they collapsed onto the tablecloth. Lying side by side, they stared contentedly into the sky, watching the fluffy white clouds drift over.

It was a long time before they spoke. "When I was a kid," Ross mused, "I'd sneak to the city park and find a place as far away from people that I could. Then I'd lie down on the grass and stare into the sky, like this, and wish I was up there in all that blue." His voice was filled with unconscious yearning.

"Take me up there, Ross—"

"Now?"

"Yes, right now." She sat up. "See that cloud?" Beside her, Ross caught the excitement in her voice and sat up. "I want to catch that cloud!" Gloria exclaimed. "I want to touch it and hold on to it before it disappears forever." She turned and looked into Ross's eyes that were even bluer than the sky above them. "We don't have much time."

"No, we don't." Ross knew they were not speaking of the cloud. "Let's hurry," he responded with excitement.

It took mere minutes to pack up and stow their picnic supplies in the Stearman.

"You take the pilot's seat," Ross said as they started to climb aboard. "I'll fly copilot. You landed this baby. Now you can take her up; and no arguments."

Gloria grinned. "Aye, aye, Captain—I mean, Major." She pulled on her leather helmet and climbed lithely into the rear seat.

"Ross—" He turned from his seat up front. "This is turning out to be the best day of my life."

"Mine too," he agreed and kissed her until she was breathless.

"Stop that, Ross," she sighed, "or I'll be too dizzy to fly."

"Why do you think I'm flying copilot, Doc?" Eyes sparkling, he settled himself in the forward cockpit.

Gloria's first takeoff was as successful as her first landing. For several hours they explored the Virginia skies, drifting with the clouds, content to have the world to themselves.

"Look, Ross! That lake—" She tilted the plane to the left to give Ross a better view. "The land on its northern shore is my father's old farm. My brother and I used to fish in the lake, even though we weren't supposed to." She laughed softly into the radio.

"Fresh fish would be great fried in that cornmeal from the mill," Ross murmured. "Gloria, put us down in that pasture, there, just beyond those poplars."

"We don't have any fishing gear—"

"Leave that to me. Let's see you do a three-point landing."

"You don't think I can do it, do you?" She banked the plane easily in the proper direction.

The landing was not a three-point but admirable enough to satisfy Gloria. Ross congratulated her as they jumped to the ground.

"You're not really going fishing?" she asked as they eased their parched throats with iced tea from the thermos.

"And waste perfectly good cornmeal?" Ross set his paper cup on the wing and leaped onto the foot board. From behind the pilot's seat, he produced a nondescript plastic box.

"My survival kit," he explained, rejoining Gloria on the ground. He opened the box. "Ahh, here it is." He held up a shiny metal fishhook. "Now we need this." He produced a flat plastic bag with a coil of nylon cord. "And this." Another bag held an assortment of lead weights. "I don't always use these to fish with—they're great for holding down a survival blanket."

"Ross, we can't fish in that lake. The man who lives on the next farm always chased us kids off. With a shotgun. As far as I know, he still owns the place and considers the lake his exclusive property."

"That shotgun didn't scare you and your brother off."

"Oh, yes, it did. In all those years we never got one trout!"

"Come on, then. I'll show you the secret." Taking her hand, he urged her to keep up with him.

The two-acre lake was a clear blue, its grassy shores shaded by thick stands of willow. Ross looked up and down the shore. "Over there." He led Gloria to an outcropping of moss-covered rocks that edged a deep pool of water. "Quiet now. Don't want to scare any trout out of that grassy bottom. I've got them where I want 'em!"

He helped Gloria find a ringside seat on the rocks. "Wait here." He retraced a few steps. Bending, he pried a rock from the damp earth. Gloria grimaced as he held up a wriggling earthworm. Back at the edge of the pool, Ross attached the worm to the hook and lowered it into the water.

"I don't believe you're doing this," Gloria whispered.

"Shh! You'll scare off that trout!"

"I don't see any—oh!" Sure enough, she caught sight of a sleek trout feeding in the long grasses growing at the bottom of the pool.

"Don't let him see our shadows," Ross warned in a low voice and Gloria froze.

Within a few minutes, the nylon line went taut. "He's a big one!" Getting to his feet, he wrestled with the fish struggling at the other end of line. "It's times like this I wish for a rod and reel!" he remarked puffing.

As he lifted the makeshift fishing apparatus out of the water, the fish flashed angrily in the sunlight.

"Oh, baby, you'll look great in a frying pan!" Ross practically smacked his lips.

"Ross!" Gloria stood up and, hands on hips, glared at the triumphant fisherman. "You're not really going to eat him!"

"That was the general idea."

"But you can't! He's so beautiful and . . and . . ."

"And fat. Perfect for dinner."

"Ross Adams, we're going to have to talk. I never really thought you'd catch anything."

Ross rolled his eyes dramatically. "Now you tell me."

A scratchy voice interrupted their exchange of words. "Hello, there! I thought I heard voices!"

"Oh, my God!" Gloria whispered frantically, staring past Ross's shoulder. "It's old Mr. Perry! The farmer I told you about—"

Ross did not turn around. "The one with the shotgun."

"Yes." Gloria's gaze shifted from Ross to Mr. Perry and then back again. "It's in his hand. Oh, no, the fish! We'll never get out of here alive!" Ross's eyes widened as Gloria snatched the flopping fish and stuffed it inside his leather jacket. Leaning close to Ross, she zipped the trout securely out of sight.

Ross clapped his hands to his chest. "What do you think you're doing, you crazy woman?"

"Hiding the evidence. Saving your life—you'll see," she hissed back.

Mr. Perry interrupted them once more. "That your plane I heard?"

Ross turned around. The fish struggled beneath his jacket. Frantically Gloria placed herself between the two men.

"Yes." Gloria did not give Ross a chance to answer. "Do you remember me, Mr. Perry?"

The old man in denim overalls squinted at the couple. "Well, well." He lowered the shotgun. "If it isn't Gloria Russell. Nice to see you, girl."

Ross shifted his weight, the movement bringing his chest up against Gloria's back. She felt the fish wriggling against her shoulder blades.

"Who's your friend?" Mr. Perry was asking.

"Oh! This is Major Ross Adams. He owns the biplane. I was just showing him where I grew up." Gloria was well aware that she was babbling. "We'll be out of here in no time. I hope the noise of the engine didn't bother you."

"Oh, no bother, girl. Just wanted to make sure you didn't have engine trouble."

"No, no engine trouble." Gloria's smile was wobbly.

"Good, good." The old man nodded. "Well, nice seeing you. And nice meetin' you, Major." Mr. Perry made as if to turn away. "Oh, Gloria," he said thoughtfully, "when you cook that fish for your beau tonight, be sure to use fresh cornmeal. And don't overcook it. See you folks." With a wave and a cackle of laughter, he and his shotgun disappeared into the trees.

Gloria sank limply against Ross's chest. "He knew all the time!" she gasped.

"And he didn't shoot us—"

Gloria whirled about. "Don't laugh at me, Ross Adams!" His lips twitched, his eyes glinted with humor.

"The trout!" Gloria forgot her disgruntlement as she remembered the fish. "He's not moving!"

Ross quickly unzipped his jacket and gingerly removed the trout. "Asphyxiated."

"Oh, no—" The two stared at the still fish. Gloria was the first to laugh, the sound spilling out despite herself. "Did you see how smug Mr. Perry looked?"

"You made his day, Gloria," Ross admitted, his grin widening with each second.

"I know. And he's not nearly as ferocious as I remembered."

"We'll have to send him a thank-you card for not impounding our dinner."

"You did say you were cooking?"

Ross groaned. "Don't tell me. You can't fry fish."

"Why do you think I wanted to throw him back?"

Laughing, they ran to the plane. As they took to the air, Gloria had an excellent view of the house where she had grown up. The surrounding fields, lush with green grass and newly planted crops, were incredibly beautiful. Memories of a wonderful childhood washed over her. As the plane banked to the south, Gloria realized how hard it really must have been for her father to leave his farm behind. Back at their own farmhouse, Ross and Gloria secured the Stearman in the hangar. Ross cooked dinner and Gloria praised his efforts. Pleasantly tired and happy with their day together, they parted with a lingering kiss.

In the following weeks, Ross and Gloria spent every available moment together. Gloria felt as if she'd come out of a long hibernation. Ross's world was all fresh air and lacy clouds. It was a place where she felt completely alive. Her proficiency in flying increased, and instead of trying to close out the sound of Ross's many visitors, she joined in to talk aviation.

The first weekend in May, Ross went out of town on TDY, taking a busload of students to tour an airbase in Ohio. Gloria took the opportunity to join her parents for Sunday dinner. John and Karen were there but Margie was out with Tony. After the meal, Barry took the kids outside for a game of croquet. Gloria helped her mother wash the dishes. Valerie Russell was quiet. "Are you worried about something, Mother? Is it Margie's relationship with Tony?" John had groused about the situation over dinner.

"Your sister is a grown woman," Gloria's mother replied. "I'm sure she knows what she's doing." She did not look up from scrubbing a casserole dish.

"Mother, you're going to rub the finish off that." Valerie let the dish fall back into the water.

"Oh, it's no use, Gloria." From a kitchen drawer, she pulled out a newspaper clipping. It was from the classified section. Gloria read the headline out loud, "For sale, Florida citrus grove." Her eyes widened.

"Mother, does this mean what I think it means?"

"I'm trying to get up enough courage to show this to your father. He was so insistent on leaving the farm—he kept talking about how I deserved a better life, more security—but, to tell you the truth, I miss farming. There was a challenge to life then, the excitement of pitting yourself against nature. Of course, I'm older now and I can't take the cold weather as well as I used to. Then a few weeks ago I saw this ad for a grove in Florida for sale. It's been in the back of my mind ever since."

Gloria scanned the details of the ad. "It does sound interesting. And you're not exactly over the hill."

Valerie laughed, then quickly sobered. "Did I hear a vote of confidence from my daughter—the same daughter who hated depending on the seasons for a livelihood?"

"That was me." Slowly she formulated the words she thought she'd never say. "I was out at the farm the other day—with Ross. When we flew overhead, I realized something. It was a mistake for Dad to sell the farm. He hasn't been the same since. And neither have you."

"Oh, Gloria." Valerie scrutinized her daughter's face. "I didn't think you'd noticed."

"I hadn't. Until recently." Her admission made her realize how far she'd come since the day Ross Adams had landed in her backyard and expanded her horizons.

Her mother seemed to read her thoughts. "It's Ross, isn't it? You've fallen in love."

"Yes, I have." It was Gloria's turn to concentrate on the casserole dish. "Not that anything will come of it. He has strong convictions. As long as he flies fighter planes, he won't let a woman into his life...and..."

"Yes?"

"Even if he would, I'd never ask him to give up his flying. He'd end up like you and Dad, living a life you really don't want to live." Gloria looked into her mother's eyes. "Ross and I don't have a future—but you and Dad do. I say show Dad the article and tell him how you feel."

Barry peeked into the kitchen. "How you feel about what?" The two women exchanged a quick glance.

"I'm suddenly in the mood for a rousing game of croquet," Gloria said and slipped out of the room, leaving her parents alone.

Chapter Eleven

A few weeks later Valerie and Barry left for Florida. Gloria was happy to see her parents infused with new energy and zest for life. She felt the same way. Her relationship with Ross had given her a new perspective on life in general. When she wasn't at her computer, she was helping Ross with preparations for the upcoming fly-in.

When the first wave of biplanes touched down on a Friday afternoon in late April, Gloria was working at her desk. Alerted by the sound, Gloria went to her window. Ross was on hand, greeting the newly arrived aviators with great enthusiasm. He and a tall man with dark brown hair clapped one another on the back. Catching sight of Gloria in the window, Ross beckoned.

"This is Lt. Col. Warner George," Ross announced as she joined the men on the field. "He's a member of my unit in Florida. Warner, Gloria Russell. She lives in the apartment below mine."

"I've seen your picture," Gloria told Warner as they shook hands. She remembered his face from one of the photographs on Ross's bookcase.

"You drag that thing around with you?" Warner gave Ross a sidelong glance.

"I always was a glutton for punishment."

"Then why am I the one sleeping out on the lawn in a tent?" Warner bantered with his friend.

"Do you need help setting things up?" Gloria offered.

"No," he answered, "but after the tent is pitched, I could always use some company." Thick dark brows jiggled up and down in mock invitation.

"No, thanks, Warner. I've heard all about you fighter pilots," Gloria teased. "But if you need a shower, you're welcome to use my bathroom."

"Thanks," Warner replied. "I think."

As the men turned to pitching tents, Gloria went back to her apartment to take care of a variety of chores.

An hour later Ross sought her out. Transfixed, he halted in the kitchen doorway to watch the small slender woman working at the kitchen counter. With her dark hair clipped at the nape of her neck, she looked young and vulnerable, more of a girl than the capable woman she was. A warm glow spread through him and quickly heated his blood.

If only he could have one night with her! It was a forbidden thought, and he pushed it from his mind. Loving her in the true sense of the word would create bonds between them—bonds that would tie him down.

Despite himself, Ross sought the warmth of Gloria's touch. "I already miss being alone with you." Slipping up behind her, he wrapped his arms around her waist. His cheek sought the sleekness of her hair. A sense of belonging settled over him, and he closed his eyes. It was such an everyday thing, ordinary really, a man coming into a kitchen to put his arms around his woman. When he was with Gloria he never wanted to leave her, yet he spent many a private hour reminding himself that soon, too soon, he would have to. In the meantime, he wanted to touch her, hold her, memorize the feel of her in his arms.

Gloria turned. "You're having the time of your life out there."

"Yeah, but that doesn't mean I can't miss you."

"I'm not going anywhere. Well, only as far as the barbecue pit. Are you hungry?"

Smooth white teeth scraped gently along the curve of her neck. "For hamburgers, I mean." She laughed breathlessly.

Ross raised his head. "You're cooking?"

"Not exactly. I made potato salad. You're going to cook these." She reached for a platter piled high with meat patties. Ross reluctantly allowed her to slip out of his arms.

"Did you get the tents pitched?"

"Come see for yourself." The sun was low on the horizon as Ross carried the platter of meat outside. Gloria followed with a packet of sesame seed buns and the potato salad. Trestle tables and benches were set up to one side of the barbecue pit where three charcoal fires flamed. A half-dozen biplane owners, including Warner, lounged on lawn chairs arranged in a loose circle. Cheery greetings welcomed Ross and Gloria.

The fly-in was a yearly event, a time to renew old acquaintances, an event to celebrate the joy of flight and exchange ideas on the maintenance and restoring of the Stearman biplanes. The subject dominated the evening's conversation.

Bonfires were lit, marshmallows roasted and much laughter filled the night air. When the visitors sang bawdy war songs, Gloria laughed at the lyrics. Sitting on the cool ground with Ross's arms wrapped loosely around her shoulders, she fell asleep, her head resting naturally on his strong broad shoulder.

The remainder of the club arrived Saturday morning, along with an assortment of students and townfolk, all anxious to see the vintage planes up close.

Gloria was watching touch and go's at the edge of the runway when a familiar voice spoke to her. "I hope I'm welcome." Erik Windom's question was a tentative one.

"Of course you are!" Gloria gave him a hug. "You've stayed away too long."

"I've been busy." It was a lame excuse. "The truth is, I saw Margie and she said you were seeing the major. Is it serious?"

Gloria drew in a deep breath. "Not on his part." Her eyes followed a plane rolling down the airstrip.

Like her, Erik watched the brightly painted aircraft rise over the poplars at the far end of the field. "I was afraid this would happen."

Gloria whirled to face her friend. "Don't feel sorry for me, Erik Windom!" she said in a strong voice. "Knowing Ross has been wonderful! I won't regret one minute of the time I'm spending with him. Why, just look at this place!" Her eyes skimmed the busy surroundings. "It's alive!"

"And noisy!" Erik winced as another plane lumbered into the air, its rumbling sound almost drowning out their words.

Pilots took orderly turns at taking off and landing. Scattered like colorful dragonflies around the hangar were a half-dozen more Stearmans in various stages of readiness. Enthusiastic aviators crowded around disassembled engines. Tools and repair manuals cluttered wing spans. The farm had never seen so much excitement.

Erik wandered off to inspect a plane he found particularly interesting. People from the local area filtered in all day long, and the place took on the air of a country fair. A reporter from the campus newspaper snapped pictures and interviewed pilots who had come from as far away as Texas and Maine. Gloria overheard Ross explaining that the Stearman biplanes had been built in the mid 1930s and had been used by the army and navy as training aircraft.

In the afternoon, Margie and Tony showed up together. Karen and John tagged reluctantly behind, as if to make certain their displeasure over their mother's choice of companion was duly noted. Their moodiness evaporated when Ross waved them toward his plane. After that it was easy for Gloria's niece and nephew to keep their distance from Tony until it was time for the foursome to leave hours later.

"Can I persuade you to take a spin in my plane?"Warner George regarded Gloria with smiling green eyes. Of all Ross's friends, he was most like Ross, a born leader, a man with charisma and intelligence to match. And Gloria liked his lopsided smile.

"You don't even have to twist my arm, Warner. Ross says that you're the finest pilot he knows."

"Will I have to answer to Ross if I spirit you into the skies?" Shrewd eyes studied her reaction.

She laughed. "No, I'm my own person. Besides, Ross is the one who introduced me to flying. It would serve him right if I ran away with the first good-looking guy who asks me!"

"Oh, lady, you're talking my language!"

Laughing like old friends, they made their way to the edge of the field where his red-and-blue 1937 Stearman waited. Warner showed her the modifications he'd made to the engine before they took their place in line for takeoff.

As they rolled down the airstrip, Gloria caught sight of Ross. He waved to her and Warner and watched them take to the air.

It was late Saturday night before Gloria and Ross saw each other again. Her hair wet from a shower, she was ready to snap out the light and go to bed when he knocked on her door.

"Why is it we always seem to meet in your kitchen?" Ross shut the door behind him.

"It certainly can't be the lure of my cooking." Gloria was happy to see him. "Sit down. The tea is still hot." By the time he propped himself in a kitchen chair, she was setting a mug of hot dark liquid in front of him.

Ross captured her hand before she could move away. "I can't sleep at night, Gloria."

"You've been busy with the fly-in...."

A quick shake of his head denied her theory. "It's thinking of you down here, wearing that flimsy nightie—" The dimness of the room did not prevent Ross's eyes from finding her curves beneath the semitransparent fabric. It was the same gown she'd worn the night of the recall.

"Would you feel better if I switched to pajamas?" she teased.

"Not really. Well, maybe if they were my pajamas. Or at least the top—"

"Be serious."

"I am." Ross pulled her onto his lap. "Put your arms around my neck, Gloria."

"Like this?" She liked the feel of his nape beneath her fingers.

"Yes. Now rest your head on my shoulder."

"This way?"

"Umm-hmm. Now run your fingers through my hair."

She raised her head and peered into his face. "You're very good at giving orders, Major. How good are you at taking them?" Her question was deliberately provocative.

"I was the top of the class at OTS."

The challenge in his voice made her heart stop beating. Her breath caught in her chest. "What does OTS mean in real English?"

His eyes held her enthralled. "Officer Training School. But you were speaking of giving orders. I'm ready and waiting."

"Tilt your head." She cupped one hand around his jaw. "Like this." He cooperated fully. "Now close your eyes." Gold-tipped lashes fluttered down, fanning his rugged cheeks.

"No fair peeking!" Gloria warned and closed the space between their lips. His mouth opened, eagerly accepting her touch. Gloria wrapped her arms around Ross's neck. Their kiss was a hungry one.

"You can give me orders anytime you like, Doc." Ross was breathing hard.

Her own voice was a rough whisper. "Kiss me, Ross. Kiss me again. . . ."

He did and a delicious warmth flooded through her. Ross's hand traced a length of shapely leg, his fingers slipping beneath the hem of her nightie. Her legs went weak and a hot wind rushed across her lower limbs. His other hand moved along the line of her spine, pressing her upper torso to his.

Eager masculine lips released hers, only to find their way downward along her neck and across the delicate curve of her collarbone. His seeking mouth discovered the taut peak of one breast, his tongue working indescribable magic as it dampened the fabric.

Her hands clasped his head, holding him close to the valley between her tingling breasts. "Ross, I think it's time to—" A knock at the kitchen door made Gloria jerk away from him.

Ross muttered an expletive beneath his breath. Smoothing down her gown, Gloria took refuge behind the chair while Ross got the door.

"Warner," he growled. "Your timing is the pits."

"Oh, sorry—I can come back later." Gloria saw the towel hanging around Warner's neck and she remembered offering him the use of her bathroom.

"No problem, Warner," she called. "Ross was just leaving. Go ahead and have your shower." Her voice was remarkably calm, considering the riot of sensations in her body. "I, uh, I have some work to catch up on in my office." It wasn't true, but it was the only thing she could think of saying. "See you two tomorrow."

Sunday morning brought a stiff breeze and overcast skies, grounding all planes for a few hours. The aviators packed their belongings, checked wing tanks and exchanged ideas over hot coffee and mountains of doughnuts.

By noon the skies cleared to partly cloudy and some of the pilots took the opportunity to head home. By midafternoon, only a handful of Ross's friends were left, including Warner George. Then Warner was the only one left.

Ross and Gloria saw him off together, watching the aircraft gain speed as it roared down the airstrip. Warner would fly only as far as North Carolina that afternoon, stopping off to stay the night with family.

The 1937 Stearman took to the air easily, then banked and turned to buzz the field. Arm in arm, Ross and Gloria waved. Then the unbelievable happened.

Warner's plane seemed to lurch and tilt, and before Gloria could assimilate the signals, the plane plunged into a thick grove of trees a quarter mile beyond the farm.

Ross reacted immediately. "Gloria. Gloria, listen to me—" Shocked brown eyes clung to Ross's face. "Run to the phone. Run, do you understand?" Mutely she nodded. "Call the paramedics, the fire department." He gave her a slight push, then he was off in the direction of the crash site.

Later the episode seemed like a dream to Gloria. Sirens split the air, medics were everywhere. Ross was white faced and calm as he told Gloria he would ride in the ambulance with Warner—Warner who was still, so thin looking beneath a white sheet.

Zombielike, Gloria huddled on the couch in her living room to wait for Ross's return. It was after midnight when she heard a car pull into the driveway. A door slammed and the vehicle pulled back onto the street. Footsteps on Ross's stairs told her it was him.

Not turning on any lights, she darted up the stairs after him. His door was standing wide open. Against the single light of the brass lamp, she saw the slump of his shoulders, the weary tilt of his head. He was holding the photograph of Warner.

Ross turned. Gloria went to him, wrapping her arms tightly about his rigid torso.

"How is he?" She feared the worst.

"He'll make it—"

"It was close?"

"Too close." Ross's lips formed a grim line.

"Oh, Ross." She gazed into his face. "I was so worried about you."

Gloria felt him freeze. "What?"

Loving eyes searched his taut features. "I was worried about you," she repeated.

Strong hands went to her arms, his fingers circling the delicate flesh just above her elbows. He held her away from him. "I don't want you to worry about me, Gloria." There was a bleakness in his eyes.

"I couldn't help it! I kept thinking if that had been you out there—"

His fingers tightened on her arms. "You forgot it was dangerous, didn't you?" Now anger flashed in his eyes. "Flying is great fun. Daring, exhilarating, and you always landed safely. And that's the problem!"

His grip hurt her arms but she scarcely noticed. All she knew was that his blue eyes had taken on a glacial hue.

Ross continued. "Once you forget that flying is a dangerous occupation, you start running into trouble. You increase your chances of making a mistake. A fatal mistake!'' His face an angry mask, he pushed her away from him. ''You forgot that. I forgot that!''

Confusion muddled Gloria's already frayed senses. ''First you tell me not to worry about you, then you tell me to remember that flying is dangerous. Ross, I can't do both!''

When he didn't answer, she cried out, ''What is it you want from me?''

''Want!'' The word was an explosion of sound and he turned burning eyes on her. ''Nothing! I don't want anything from you.'' He lowered his voice and repeated the words. ''I don't want anything at all, Gloria. In four weeks my assignment here will be complete and I'll be out of here.'' He spoke like an automaton. ''I'll look back on our friendship as a pleasant few months, a fun interlude in our lives, after which we both went our separate ways.''

Gloria's heart sank, yet she knew full well that what he said was true. In four weeks they would say goodbye. Reality spurred her on to something she'd been contemplating for weeks. But he interrupted her.

''Look, Gloria.'' Ross took several steps away from her. ''All I want to do right now is to go to bed.''

She followed and reached out to touch his shoulder. ''Ross.'' Her voice was a soft whisper in the night. ''You don't have to go to bed alone.''

He whirled around as if he'd been burned by a hot poker. ''You're crazy!''

''I'm crazy about you. And I don't think you should be alone right now. Ross, I love you. I didn't want to fall in love, but it's happened. And I want you to love me.'' It was painful to admit her innermost desire.

"But I... I can't!" The blue eyes were filled with anguish.

"Why not? Oh, Ross!" A thought occurred to her. "Ross, is there something you haven't told me about... an old war injury or..."

His laugh broke the tension in the room. "That's one of the things I like about you, Doc. That sweet, caring part of you." The blue eyes were no longer glacial.

She tried to smile at his word choice. "I thought it was my desirable body you liked."

"Oh, I like it all right, but..." Tension flared once more. "We have no future, Gloria."

"I'm not asking for a future, Ross. I only want one night. Or two or three before you go on your way—alone—no strings to hold you back." At the stubborn set of his chin and the thinning of his lips, a kind of anger rose in Gloria's chest. "An ideal situation, I thought." They glared at each other, Ross standing mute and unchanging.

His rejection hurt. "Ross Adams, you came into my life and turned it upside down—you and your friends making noise all hours of the day and night so I couldn't get my work done! Oh, you're all charm, you with your dashing red scarf! That's your way, isn't it? You wing your way into people's lives, you win them over and give them ideas. Then, when they want to do something about those ideas, you turn and run!" She was breathless and pale but her eyes flamed with emotion.

She'd hit a nerve. "I am not running!" But the tormented look in the eyes she loved told her otherwise. "God!" he went on a bit too quickly, "I can't blame you for being angry. Whatever you think, I am not running out of here. I laid it on the line the day we met. I never led you on, Gloria. I told you that I'm not the marrying kind!"

Anger turned to sheer fury. "Ohh!" Gloria fumed. "Listen here, buster! I never said anything about marriage!" In a flash, it hit her. "That's it! You're afraid!" As she spoke she advanced on him, closing the gap he'd put between them. She cut off his effort to reply. "You're afraid you might find yourself making a commitment to another person. Ross Adams, you are nothing but a coward in...in the Red Baron's clothing!"

"That's ridiculous!" Ross was defiant. "I go up every day and risk my life—look at what nearly happened to Warner!"

"Oh, you're fine up in the air where it's just you and your plane. You can handle that. It's on the ground that you're a washout!" Her blazing brown eyes rendered him speechless. "You act so noble, so self-sacrificing, mouthing platitudes that a man in your position has no business with a wife and family!"

Her voice dropped dramatically. "You know what, Ross Adams? You were just a kid when you went to Vietnam. But you never grew up. You can make all the excuses you want—the one about not wanting to offer a woman a life of hardship and sacrifice is a great one. But it's a bunch of bull! The real truth is that you're not strong enough, not man enough to handle a risky career and the responsibility of a family." She took a deep calming breath. Ross glared at her, his face contorted with suppressed emotion.

Her eyes softened. "It's so sad, Ross. You don't have anything to come home to except a machine. And if you ever make that dreaded fatal mistake in the sky, there won't be anyone but strangers at your funeral. No wife to mourn your loss, no children to carry on your name. No one to remember how wonderful you really are." Her voice broke.

"Gloria—"

"No!" Anger cut off the tears. "I don't want to hear any more excuses. I have my own machine to turn to! All I want to do is go to my office and put my life back the way it was before you came."

"I'm sorry you feel that way." His voice was a strangled sound. "What if I told you that I can't make love to you because I'm half in love with you al—"

Sad brown eyes cut him off. "I'd say you're a bigger coward than I thought." Gloria turned and walked out of the room.

Ross stared after her. He'd arrived on restless wings, searching for something intangible, like the clouds he and Gloria had chased together. He'd found what he'd been needing, a source of peace and happiness. And she'd just stripped his soul bare.

Chapter Twelve

The end of a friendship is always painful, but Gloria did not expect the depth of pain or the sweeping sense of loss that overcame her after her showdown with Ross. Warner came home from the hospital, staying in Ross's apartment and supervising salvage operations on his mangled Stearman. And then he, too, was gone, on his way back to his air force duties in Florida. After the new year, Warner would be going with Ross to the Pacific.

The elder Russells returned with ecstatic plans for the orange grove they'd bought. Their move would be accomplished in three months, giving them time to sell their house in town. Gloria was happy to see her parents looking so young and alive. It gave her an idea of what they must have been like together before their large, time-consuming family had come along.

Even Margie's life was on a fairly even keel, although she and Tony had not publicly talked about marriage. As soon as the kids adjusted to Tony's presence in their lives, Gloria was certain there would be a wedding in the family.

May turned into June altogether too quickly. As soon as finals and graduation ceremonies were completed, Ross would take Jane and the Stearman and fly away. He hadn't taken the aircraft up since Warner's accident. The hangar door remained locked, and the grass on the runway was going to seed. It was almost as if Ross Adams had never come to Blacksburg.

Only at night, when Gloria lay in bed staring at the ceiling, did she notice his presence. Above her, there was an occasional creak in the floorboards, the sound of running water or the scrape of a chair.

Once in a great while they ran into each other in the mudroom. They exchanged a mute "Hello" or a hastily murmured "Excuse me." A sad ending to a wonderful romance, Gloria thought, and yet she knew she would never apologize for her angry words.

A week before graduation, she finished her research and she delivered the hefty document to her department head. Walking outside, she was overcome with a great sense of pride and not a little amount of relief that it was over.

On the way home she stopped to see her parents, whose house was filled with packed boxes. Waving aside her offer to help, they congratulated her and sent her on her way with orders to relax. Impulsively Gloria stopped at a florist and treated herself to a bouquet of fresh flowers. She picked up a bottle of California champagne at the grocery store. Not wanting to celebrate alone, she called Margie. There was no answer, only the recording machine for Carter Realty.

Standing in her office window, she poured herself a glass of champagne. The sky had turned from an ordinary blue to a leaden gray. To match her mood, she mused, staring at the growing storm. Fat drops of rain splattered against the windowpanes.

After a bit more bubbly wine, Gloria started to enjoy the turbulent weather. She was safe behind glass, insulated from the real world, surrounded by all that was familiar to her. A blank-screened computer, a silent printer, an empty desk top. The room had always given her a feeling of security. So why did it feel like a prison of her own making?

The shrill ring of the telephone made her jump. Picking up the receiver, she spilled champagne on the carpet.

"Gloria!" Margie's voice was tightly controlled. "Thank God you're there!"

"Where else would I be? I was here yesterday and I'll be here tomorrow and the day after and the day after that—"

"Gloria," Margie interrupted her sister. "Tony and I have announced our wedding plans."

Gloria held up her glass. "That's good news, Margie. I'll drink a toast to the bride and groom—"

Again Margie cut her off. "This is not the time to celebrate."

"Sure it is! I just handed in my manuscript. Mom and Dad have rediscovered a life they love. And you and Tony are going to live happily ever after."

"Gloria, are you drunk?"

"No, but I wish I were."

"So do I. I wish this was all a bad dream and I'd wake up and find out everything was fine."

It was a thought she recognized. "Hey, wait a minute. Getting married to Tony is a bad dream? I think I missed something."

"John has run away."

"Oh, no—" The slight effect of the champagne vanished, and Gloria was stone-cold sober.

"Is he there, Gloria?"

"I haven't seen him, but there are plenty of places he could hide out around here. I'll start looking."

"Tony and I will be right over."

Champagne forgotten, Gloria checked the seldom-used front door. Finding it locked, she went from room to room, not expecting to find John but not willing to overlook anything.

The hangar! She caught sight of it through the kitchen window. The sky had darkened and clouds rolled across the horizon. In the distance, lightning flashed. Grabbing a windbreaker, Gloria darted through the mudroom and ran straight into Ross, arriving home from work. He wore his lightweight short-sleeved summer uniform.

"What is it?" He blocked her way.

"It's John! Margie and Tony announced that they are getting married and John ran away. I was just going to check the hangar." It was the first time in weeks that they'd exchanged more than three words at a time.

"I'll go with you."

She did not object, and together they checked out the Stearman, the loft and the two small storage rooms at the rear of the hangar.

As they stood in the open hangar door, ignoring the buffeting winds, Margie and Tony drove up.

"He's not here," Gloria informed her sister.

"Mom and Dad haven't seen him, either. I knew he'd be upset, but I never thought he'd go to this extreme." Tears swam in Margie's eyes. She buried her head in Tony's shoulder, seeking comfort from the man she'd chosen to be her husband.

Over Margie's head, Ross and Tony exchanged ideas. Ross asked about several friends he'd heard John mention. "What about Joey?"

Margie shook her head. "Joey's away on a camping trip."

"A camping trip—" Ross went suddenly still. "Listen, Margie, I have an idea where John might be."

"What do you mean?"

"It's just something John said the first time I took him and Karen up in the Stearman. There's a cabin up by the Cascades—"

"Oh, my God, yes. He talks about it all the time. But it takes hours to get there and you can only reach it on foot."

"Or airplane."

The three stared at Ross. "I'm going to take a look-see," he announced.

Gloria grabbed his arm just as he was turning away. "Not in this weather! The wind, and the lightning!"

"Exactly. If John hasn't been able to find the cabin, he could be trapped out in the storm. We could lose him to hypothermia." His gaze probed hers, and she knew there was nothing she could do to change his mind. Ross turned to Tony. "Call the highway patrol. I'll use my radio and make contact with the control tower at the Blacksburg airport. If I spot John, I'll try to land. If not, I'll radio his location in."

Tony raced to the phone. Gloria followed with Margie. Settling her sister at the kitchen table, she rushed back outside.

The Stearman's dependable engine cranked to life. Ross climbed into the cockpit. Gloria raised her voice to be heard over the wind.

"Ross, don't go! It's too dangerous."

Vivid blue eyes softened as they touched her face. "I have to go." She knew that what he said was true. It was one of those things he had to do. It was what set him apart from other men. It was what made her love him.

The Stearman started to move. "Ross Adams," she called out to him over the noise of the prop. "If you don't come back in one piece, I'll . . . I'll never forgive you!" Her eyes, dark and intense, were filled with all the love she felt.

Ross's return glance was inscrutable. Blinking back tears, Gloria slapped the side of the fuselage. "Go on, get this bucket of bolts out of here!"

Ross, helmeted against the elements, tossed her a final salute and taxied onto the airstrip. Wind whipped the tops of the trees and laid the grass flat. Tony appeared at Gloria's side just as the Stearman took to the air. It lurched slightly and Gloria cried out. Then the biplane overcame the forces of wind and gravity and cleared the trees with just inches to spare. The sound of the storm drowned out the roar of the Whirlwind engine, and then Ross was gone, hidden by the dark cloud cover.

"Your father's going to the airport control tower," Tony told her. "We'll wait here for word." Together they went inside.

The next hour was the longest sixty minutes Gloria had ever lived. When the phone call came, she watched her sister collapse in tears.

"Ross spotted John huddled on a plateau east of the Cascades. There's no way he can land up there, but he managed to drop John a bundle of supplies—a waterproof sleeping bag and one of those survival blankets. The highway patrol is joining up with a forester who knows the area." Tony related everything. "They want us to meet them at the ranger station," he added to Margie.

Margie turned to her sister. "Will you be okay?"

"Yes." They hugged. "I'll wait here for Ross."

"Don't give up." This from Margie.

"I won't. Not this time." And then Gloria was alone again, with time to think about what she would say to Ross when he came back to her.

And he would come back. He would thwart the winds that could smash the Stearman into unrecognizable fragments. There had been something in his eyes when he'd looked at her....

It was close to sundown when a sound just beneath the threshold of the storm caught her attention. Grabbing a flashlight, she ran outside, ignoring the pelting rain as she made her way to the airstrip.

It terrified her to think about how Ross would land in the limited visibility. The sound of the engine came again. Gloria strained her eyes to see through the storm. Looking up, she caught sight of the Stearman. It was coming in at the wrong angle.

The dying light of the sun broke through a patch of clouds and illuminated the aircraft. The bright yellow wings fluttered from side to side as the plane fought for control. It dropped altitude too fast. Gloria watched as all three wheels hit the ground. One wing scraped the grass. Then miraculously the aircraft righted itself and rolled to a halt. The engine went silent and the propellor rotated to a slow stop.

A black cloud obliterated any remaining light. Gloria snapped on the flashlight. In its beam, she caught sight of Ross jumping to the ground. Slowly, as if he had all the time in the world, he walked toward her, peeling off his helmet and goggles. The red scarf fluttered around his neck.

He came to a halt in front of her and she lowered the flashlight. "My beacon in the dark. I should have known it was you."

"I was worried about you." Her chin came up defiantly.

"I know."

"Aren't you going to tell me I shouldn't worry?"

"No. I know it wouldn't do any good."

"You're damned right it wouldn't!" Neither paid any attention to the forces of nature raging all around them. They had their own private storm to settle.

A crooked smile curved Ross's lips. "You were right about me, Doc. I'm a coward. I'm afraid to make a commitment to a woman. Truth is, it scares the hell out of me." The blue eyes were shadowed. He stepped forward and the glow of the light from the flashlight played across his weather-ravaged features.

"But I want to try, Gloria. With you, if you'll have me." She didn't speak but breathlessly waited for the right words from him. "I love you, Doc, with all my heart, but I knew that before Warner's crash." His eyes were wide and vulnerable. "When I was up there today, looking for John, fighting the wind, dodging lightning bolts, it was the thought of you waiting for me that gave me the strength to make my way home."

Gloria's hand went to his lips, halting his words. "Ross." She spoke with great difficulty. "Don't say that if you don't mean it."

He took her hand in his and kissed her fingers. "I mean it! With all my heart! I'll resign my commission and get a job here in Virginia."

Gloria's eyes caressed his face as she made her decision. "I won't be here."

"What?"

"I have other things in mind—Florida in June, somewhere in the Pacific come January."

"Oh, Gloria—"

"You'd hate it away from the job you love, Ross. You were meant to fly."

"What about your job—the tenure you've worked so hard to get? I can't ask you to give up your security."

"There are different kinds of security, Ross." She'd had her own fears to work through. "There's a great big world out there. Jobs like mine are everywhere. And besides—" she took a deep breath "—tenure in your arms is all I want."

Then she was where she wanted to be, in his arms, holding him close, touching him, making sure he was safe.

"Oh, Doc, I've been such a fool—"

"Shh—"

"It won't be easy for us."

"I never doubted that."

"You'll have to join the OWC."

"Oh, my God, what's that?"

"The Officers' Wives Club."

"Ross Adams, are you proposing?"

"You bet I am!"

"Well, I've heard about officers' wives." She bit her lower lip as if to give the matter great thought. "But I'll marry you, anyway."

A bolt of lightning lit the sky and illuminated their faces. "You're cold and dripping wet!" Ross exclaimed.

"So are you."

"What are we waiting for?" Ross exclaimed. "It's out of those clothes and into a hot bath and warm bed." They started to run toward the house.

Gloria tugged Ross's hand and he slowed down. "Major Adams, I love you."

"Dr. Russell, I love you." Hand in hand they raced across the dark field, the wind in their faces and hope in their hearts.

COMING NEXT MONTH

#514—THE THINGS WE DO FOR LOVE—Glenda Sands

When pretty Shelby Thurston offered Austin Hastings ready employment, he was intrigued enough to accept. Little did the handsome engineer know the talents the job entailed. But he would do anything for love—and Shelby.

#515—TO CHOOSE A WIFE—Phyllis Halldorson

Susan Alessandro was a blond angel, but Marco Donatello had never been attracted to innocent romantics, especially one his father had handpicked for him to marry. They had nothing in common—except their growing love for each other.

#516—A DANGEROUS PROPOSITION—Melodie Adams

As an undercover investigator, Blake Marlow was a professional. So why was suspected smuggler Cassandra Wyatt giving him sleepless nights? He should have been able to handle a routine case, but his unexpected feelings for Cassandra were anything but routine.

#517—MAGGIE MINE—Karen Young

Maggie Taylor believed in love, marriage and happily ever after.
Cash McKenzie was a dyed-in-the-wool cynic, disillusioned with romance. Could Maggie reawaken the romantic in Cash and teach him to love again?

#518—THE BOY NEXT DOOR—Arlene James

Ronni Champlain still cringed at the memory of her adolescent crush on Jeff Paul Logan, and she was determined to stay away from him. But when her little sister started to gaze at him with hero-worship in her eyes, Ronni knew she had to step in. Could she save her sister, or would Ronni soon fall back under Jeff Paul's magical spell?

#519—MR. LONELYHEARTS—Suzanne Forster

When Scott "The Hunter" Robinson refused to notice Amy Dwyer, she wrote to her paper's advice column for help. She was surprised to find that Hunter was the new columnist! Soon, Amy was following his advice—right into his heart.

AVAILABLE THIS MONTH:

#508 ONE OF THE FAMILY
Victoria Glenn

#509 TANGLED TRIUMPHS
Terri Herrington

#510 A MIST ON THE MOUNTAIN
Stella Bagwell

#511 PERFECT PARTNERS
Jennifer Mikels

#512 NO COMPETITION
Debbie Macomber

#513 ON RESTLESS WINGS
Mia Maxam